"I LOVE THE FEEL OF YOU,"
SHE WHISPERED HELPLESSLY . . .

Samantha was lost in a tide of sensation. Her
head pressed back into the pine boughs as
her body arched to the skilled teasing of his
lips, and she felt her nipples burst into
bloom beneath the warm circling of his
tongue. The air was cold, but Sam felt only
the fire singing through her veins as Luke's
hands curved over her hips and drew her
against him. . . .

MAGGIE OSBORNE grew up in Kansas and Colorado.
After attending college in Colorado, she worked on a
newspaper and then as a stewardess. She currently lives
with her husband and son in Colorado. In addition to
community activities, her leisure projects include painting and renovating old houses jointly with her family.

Dear Reader:

We at Rapture Romance hope you will continue to enjoy our four books each month as much as we enjoy bringing them to you. Our commitment remains strong to giving you only the best, by well-known favorite authors and exciting new writers.

We've used the comments and opinions we've heard from *you*, the reader, to make our selections, so please keep writing to us. Your letters have already helped us bring you better books—the kind you want—and we appreciate and depend on them. Of course, we are always happy to forward mail to our authors—writers need to hear from their fans!

And don't miss any of the inside story on Rapture. To tell you about upcoming books, introduce you to the authors, and give you a behind-the-scenes look at romance publishing, we've started a *free* newsletter, *The Rapture Reader*. Just write to the address below, and we will be happy to send you each issue.

Happy reading!

The Editors
Rapture Romance
New American Library
1633 Broadway
New York, NY 10019

FLIGHT OF FANCY

by

Maggie Osborne

RAPTURE ROMANCE
NEW AMERICAN LIBRARY

NAL BOOKS ARE AVAILABLE AT QUANTITY DISCOUNTS
WHEN USED TO PROMOTE PRODUCTS OR SERVICES.
FOR INFORMATION PLEASE WRITE TO PREMIUM MARKETING DIVISION,
NEW AMERICAN LIBRARY, 1633 BROADWAY,
NEW YORK, NEW YORK 10019.

SIGNET, SIGNET CLASSIC, MENTOR, PLUME, MERIDIAN AND
NAL BOOKS are published by New American Library,
1633 Broadway, New York, New York 10019

First Printing, May, 1984

1 2 3 4 5 6 7 8 9

PRINTED IN THE UNITED STATES OF AMERICA

Chapter One

~~

"I hope you don't object, Miss Adams—I've asked Luke Bannister to join us for lunch."

Sam Adams' dark head jerked upward and her eyes widened, then narrowed sharply. Damn! Luke Bannister again—the man was everywhere. And he was driving her crazy. Every time she turned around someone was singing Luke Bannister's praises. And all too often it was one of her own clients, about to transfer his business from Adams Air Freight to Bannister Air Freight.

Biting her lip, Sam glanced across the restaurant table at Bill Chilton, the client she hoped to save from Bannister's clutches.

"I don't object at all," she lied, hoping her voice sounded convincing. In fact, she objected like hell. She hadn't flown to Aspen to share her meeting with the competition; she'd come here to nail down Chilton's business.

Frowning, Sam turned the stem of her wineglass between her fingers. She couldn't afford to lose another account. The very thought raised a lump of depression in her chest. Her father had cautioned her to expect a few losses when he retired and she assumed the presidency of Adams Air—but neither of them had expected the client base to erode as badly as it had.

"We might as well wrap this up today, Miss Adams. Thought I'd hear what both of you have to say and then make my decision." Chilton signaled

the cocktail waitress and pointed to their empty
glasses. Nothing in his wide, cheerful smile indicated he saw anything awkward in inviting Sam's
biggest competitor to share their lunch.

Sam stared at the bright mountain sunshine sparkling through the autumn foliage on the trees shading the mall. Her jaw set in a stubborn line. She
didn't intend to surrender her client without a fight.

Drawing a breath, she focused a dazzling smile on
Bill Chilton. This was one account Luke Bannister
was not going to steal. "Why do you need to make a
decision, Mr. Chilton? Adams Air has handled your
business for years. In fact, you were one of my
father's first customers, if I recall correctly. May I
ask why you're considering a change now?"

"No particular reason." Chilton shrugged. "Just
figured it was time to check around a little. A man
doesn't like to find himself in a rut."

Sam suppressed a soft explosion of frustration.
Why didn't anyone tell her the truth? Why didn't
Chilton admit he wasn't convinced a twenty-seven-
year-old female could adequately operate a freight
company? She could have fought the truth and won.
She'd been her father's assistant for five years, and
for all intents and purposes she had operated Adams
Air throughout the past year, with Frank Adams
providing only minimal guidance. She was efficient,
competent, and skilled at business administration.
And she was confident that she could prove herself if
her clients would only give her the opportunity.

Folding her hands over the menu, Sam leaned forward, unwilling to accept Chilton's response. "Has
Adams Air been unsatisfactory in any way? Have we
missed a deadline, Mr. Chilton? Have we misplaced
any of your shipments?"

Chilton touched his collar and cast an uncomfortable glance toward the mall beyond the window. "No, no. Nothing like that."

"Then what? If we're doing a good job why are you considering a change? I'm afraid I don't understand."

Sam knew she was putting Chilton on the spot. And she was being more aggressive than was her usual style. But any minute Luke Bannister would walk through the door and then what? A flash of irritation sparked in her eyes. Her nerves were already on edge. She resented having Luke Bannister sitting in on her presentation.

The solution was to accomplish as much as possible before Bannister arrived. She leaned forward expectantly, silently urging Chilton to haste, waiting for his answer.

Instead, Bill Chilton sprang from his seat with an expression of decided relief and thrust out his hand. "Luke! Glad to see you. Have you met your competition, Samantha Adams?"

"I haven't had the pleasure, Bill. Hello, Samantha Adams."

Sam's heart sank. Bannister possessed an immediate advantage; he and Chilton were on a first-name basis. She quickly bolstered her flagging spirits with a reminder that this was *her* client and *her* meeting, then pushed a wave of soft brown hair behind her ear, forced her lips into a smile, and lifted her head.

A tiny gasp escaped her throat as she stared up into vibrant blue eyes warm with interest and admiration.

To Sam's dismay, Luke Bannister resembled a romantic's version of the perfect dashing pilot. A baseball cap sat atop an unruly mass of blue-black hair that was beginning to gray at temples and sideburns; one dark lock tumbled provocatively across his bronzed forehead. His jaw was square and authoritative. A wide, sensual mouth curved beneath a strong nose. Scuffed cowboy boots emerged from the bottom of low-slung jeans. Dark hair curled from his opened collar.

"How do you do," Sam murmured weakly, releasing a long breath. If Bannister had worn a mustache, she would have sworn she was looking at Clark Gable playing the role of a pilot.

Annoyed with herself, Sam decided she'd been watching too many late-night reruns. But, as God was her witness, Luke Bannister was a dead ringer for Clark Gable. That is, if Gable had possessed eyes the color of a bright morning sky.

And Bannister was certainly as devastating— from his wide shoulders to his lean, tapered waist to the casual confidence with which he drew back a chair. For reasons Sam could no longer recall, she had expected Luke Bannister to be short, paunchy, and balding. She had definitely not anticipated tall, dark, and handsome.

As that thought chased through her mind, Bannister caught her slim fingers in his large hand and pressed firmly, his blue eyes staring into hers.

"Samantha Adams," he said slowly, softly, "I hope you like the looks of me because I am going to marry you."

"I beg your pardon?"

"I'm going to marry you. I knew it the minute I walked in the door and saw you."

A pang of disappointment pushed at the polite smile pasted on Sam's lips. Against all logic, she didn't want Bannister to be superficial. A man who looked like Clark Gable shouldn't be shallow.

"Fine, Mr. Bannister. Why don't you go out and find us a preacher? I'll stay here and wrap things up with Mr. Chilton."

Luke Bannister laughed, but his steady gaze continued to caress her high cheekbones before dropping to linger teasingly on her lips. "Now that I've found you, darlin', I'm not going anywhere without you."

Sam's pained smile thinned and a sharp reply sprang to her lips—and died there. The intensity in Bannister's eyes halted her sarcasm before she could voice it.

To her utter astonishment, she experienced a confusing rush of warmth as his fingers continued to enclose her hand, and his blue, blue eyes explored her features. She couldn't recall when she'd last been subjected to such blatant speculation, if ever. Feeling an embarrassed heat rising in her cheeks, she tried to drop her eyes, but Luke Bannister's gaze held her as tightly as his grip, drawing her deeply into pools of calm blue.

Her breath quickened even as she furiously berated herself. This was utterly ridiculous. Bannister was enacting a scene straight from an ancient celluloid fantasy. Clark Gable falls instantly in love. If she believed that, she could as easily believe a Confederate soldier was going to burst into the restaurant any minute shouting: "Atlanta is burning!"

"Well, well," Bill Chilton beamed cheerfully. "I'd hoped you two would get along, but I didn't expect this."

Luke Bannister's eyes swept Sam's oval face, her dark cloud of hair, the hollow thudding at the base of her throat. "I've been waiting for you all of my life. Samantha, darlin', you are simply the most beautiful creature I've ever seen."

Sam blinked at him. Then she snatched her hand free and her brow drew into an angry frown. "May I remind you that this is a business lunch, Mr. Bannister?"

A flush of crimson stained her cheeks. She couldn't believe she had momentarily responded to a line as old as the mountains rising beyond the window. Clearly Bannister had been watching late-night TV too. Frantically, she searched her mind for a brisk, light comment to show him she wasn't affected by his clumsy attempt at charm. But the snappy retorts that usually sprang so easily to her tongue died in her throat. She glanced into his thick-lashed eyes and felt herself drowning in warm blue skies and summer days. She'd never seen eyes so blue.

"Beautiful," he repeated, seating himself across from her. To Sam's mounting confusion, Bannister continued to inspect her as if they were alone. His eyes roamed intimately from the shining gloss of her dark hair to the fullness of her cashmere-clad breasts.

Sam recognized that look and resented it. Her brown eyes flashed a warning as Bannister's smile returned to her flushed face. Men who attempted to transform business meetings into social conquests annoyed her, as did empty compliments.

Sam knew she was attractive, and she made the best of what nature had given her. But she wasn't beautiful. Her dark eyes were too widely set, her mouth too full. At five foot ten, she was too tall for most men. If Luke Bannister thought she was idiotic enough to abandon business in favor of flattery, he had another thing coming.

"You can save the charm for someone who appreciates it, Mr. Bannister," she said sweetly, then turned to Bill Chilton, who grinned at her. "I imagine Mr. Chilton would rather discuss business, don't you?"

Bannister hadn't glanced toward Chilton since he sat down. "If you're already married, we have a problem here."

The embarrassing blush intensified in Sam's cheeks, and her hands shook slightly. Bannister was trying to make a fool of her. Ignoring him, she leaned toward Chilton, irritated by his indulgent smile. "Mr. Chilton, how would you prefer to handle this? Would you like to ask us questions?"

"I have a few questions." Luke Bannister pushed his cap to the back of his dark curls and leaned an elbow on the table, resting his chin in his hand. "How soon can you get a divorce if you're married? How many children shall we have? And where do you want to live? Aspen? Or Denver? I'm flexible, I'll move to Denver, if you like, or . . ."

"Mr. Bannister, this has gone far enough!" Sam's fists clenched above the menu. The heat in her cheeks flamed into scarlet circles. "Do you think we could conduct this meeting in a professional manner?" She fervently hoped Bill Chilton was noting Bannister's wildly unprofessional approach.

"Samantha, darlin', what's more important than our future?" Bannister turned to face Chilton. "Bill, I hope you'll excuse us, but this is a red-letter day. We'll talk business another time."

"We will *not* talk business another time!" Shock and outrage choked Sam's voice. And Bill Chilton was laughing. Laughing! A sting of frustration misted her eyes. In less than five minutes Bannister had managed to turn an everyday business lunch into a mockery. He'd beaten her before they'd discussed one word of business by making her look foolish.

"Now children," Chilton said, lifting his palms. "Let's eat. Then we'll talk freight." Grinning at Bannister, he added, "After all, Miss Adams flew here from Denver just for this meeting."

"Miss Adams," Bannister repeated, smiling at her. "Glad to hear it—makes things much less complicated."

Sam's teeth ground. For a moment she considered

walking out, then realized that was exactly what Bannister wanted. If she stormed away, he would have Chilton all to himself. She looked up as Bannister eyed her soberly.

"You think this is just a line, don't you?" he asked.

"Of course."

"It's not." He leaned forward, ignoring Chilton, his blue eyes intent and holding hers against her will. "I'm a man who knows what he wants, Samantha. I always knew I'd recognize the right woman when I saw her. And you're the one, darlin'."

"Do I have anything to say about it?" Sam snapped.

He grinned. "No."

He wasn't going to stop this nonsense, she realized helplessly. Worse—some small, rebellious part of her mind was responding to him. The realization shocked her. She knew better than to believe two people could meet and instantly fall in love. Such fantasies occurred in movies, not in real life.

Releasing a small sigh, Sam clenched her fists and decided that only a pilot would attempt such an unrealistic approach. She had found pilots as a group to be outrageously confident, stubbornly independent, and totally fearless. They inhabited a small, tight world of their own making, incomprehensible to the universe at large. Though most proclaimed themselves hardheaded realists, Sam suspected they privately fancied themselves as romantic figures, adventurers, a breed apart from mortal men.

She slid a glare toward Bannister. He was better equipped than most to project the image of a dashing romantic. He was handsome and arrogant, and he transmitted a powerful masculinity that drew the glances of women at nearby tables.

Years ago Sam had resolved never to become involved with a pilot. She wanted no part of them. So why did her traitorous pulse race when Bannister stared at her as he was doing now? Disgusted with herself, she tried to recall when she'd last gazed at a man's mouth and wondered how his lips would feel pressed to hers. She hadn't entertained such a thought in years. And she didn't want to now.

"I'd like a big family, darlin', if that's agreeable. A daughter will be all right if she looks like you, but I'd appreciate it if you'd make the rest boys, because . . ."

Sam's dark eyes narrowed. "Mr. Bannister, I want you to stop this. Right now!" Flipping up her menu, she stared at it unseeing. But she continued to feel his unwavering stare, becoming more self-conscious by the minute.

What on earth was wrong with her? She was too professional for this type of reaction. She felt hot and cold at the same instant, shaky inside. She was acutely aware of Bannister's knee close to hers beneath the table. This was absolute craziness. Luke Bannister was stealing her clients; he was the enemy. And if she didn't regain control, he was going to walk off with the Chilton account.

Sam closed her eyes, then opened them and lowered the menu, smiling at the waitress. "I'll have the small steak."

"Good girl," Chilton nodded. "I like a woman who eats. Too many of them just pick at salads."

"Do you cook?" Bannister asked. "I can forgive your bad temper if you're a good cook."

Sam glared at him, then drew a determined breath. She directed a strained smile toward Chilton. "What are you looking for in a freight company, Mr. Chilton?"

"On the other hand," Bannister continued, his eyes admiring her profile, "it doesn't matter. We'll eat steaks. I can broil the best steak you ever tasted."

Bill Chilton laughed as Sam seethed. He spooned French dressing over his salad. "Rates, I guess. Dependable service . . ."

"Adams Air has provided dependable service, you said so yourself." Sam couldn't have swallowed a bite if her life depended on it. And her mouth felt peculiar. Knowing Bannister was staring at her lips made them feel wooden and strange.

Bannister had pushed away from the table and he sat with one ankle crossed over his knee, sipping coffee and steadily watching her. Sam glanced quickly at his wide mouth and then away. Under different circumstances, if he hadn't been Luke Bannister and if she hadn't been Frank Adams' daughter—maybe, just maybe, she would have enjoyed playing along with his game. But not now. Her eyes narrowed and she pushed aside her untouched salad.

"Bannister Air Freight," she said coolly, "is not noted for dependable service as I understand it." To her satisfaction, Luke Bannister sat up a little straighter. "In fact, from what I hear, Mr. Chilton, your grandson's lemonade stand is probably run more efficiently than Bannister Air Freight."

"Well, well," Chilton said cheerfully. "The little lady has teeth. What do you say to that, Luke?"

Luke Bannister grinned. "No argument. I'm a pilot, not a paperpusher." Broad shoulders shrugged beneath his light jacket. "When we're married, Sam will handle the administrative work—I've heard she's good at it. I'll supervise the pilots and fly "

He was impossible. Sam pressed her lips together and drew a breath. All right, she'd play by his stupid rules. "In case we don't get married, Mr. Chilton, and I wouldn't count on an immediate wedding, wouldn't you rather know your deadlines will be met?"

"Hold on there, darlin'." Bannister raised a large square hand. "I may not be good at paperwork, but I haven't missed a deadline yet. The freight I haul arrives on schedule." He winked at Chilton. "I'm like the post office, neither rain nor sleet nor dark of night shall delay my delivery."

"That's a poor joke, Mr. Bannister," Sam snapped. She leaned backward as the waitress placed a steak before her. "Are you admitting you fly without regard to safety?"

Bannister grinned. "I trained in Vietnam, darlin'. Which means I can fly anything, under any conditions. You gas up a toaster and I'll fly it to Chicago if that's where you want to go."

Chilton laughed. "That's what I've heard." He nodded to Sam. "Bannister has quite a reputation. He's about the best pilot you and I are ever likely to see. Tell her about the time you landed on the carrier with only one engine, Luke."

Sam listened with half an ear, her heart plummeting as she carefully studied Chilton's eager expression. Chilton didn't care about rates or schedules, he wanted the romance and adventure Bannister provided. Sam's lips pressed into a line and she stared at her plate.

Her father would have understood Bannister perfectly, Sam realized. Frank Adams would have jumped into the conversation with stories of his own dating back to World War II. Maybe that's what it took to succeed in this business, a love affair with flying. Sam shuddered lightly. She was more interested in what went inside the planes than in the planes themselves. Maybe that was her problem.

"Very interesting," she commented politely when Bannister finished his tale. "Now, about rates, Mr. Chilton . . ."

Chilton looked distinctly disappointed to return to business.

Sam continued doggedly, determined not to give

up. She turned her dark eyes on Bannister. "How do you charge? By the load or by the mile?"

Bannister laughed. "I'll show you mine if you'll show me yours."

A rush of heat colored Sam's cheeks. Furious, she bent to her briefcase and let her hair swing forward to hide her expression. She removed a sheet of paper and pushed it toward Bannister. At the last moment she realized she had allowed her annoyance to color her judgment. Her client should be receiving the rate schedule, not her competition.

Bannister scanned the page. "Whatever she charges, Bill, I'll undercut it by ten percent."

Sam gasped. "That's unethical!" Stammering, she looked from Bannister to Chilton and back again. "How can you do that?" Her hands lifted as her heart sank to her toes. The account was lost, she knew it. She'd known it from the moment Luke Bannister strode confidently into the restaurant.

"I can do it, darlin', because I'm the new kid in town. I don't have the established clientele that you have. If I'm going to stay in the air I need some customers." Bannister smiled at her, his blue eyes apologetic. "That's how it is."

She sat as still as stone, staring at him. Then she looked at Bill Chilton and knew from his expression what his decision was. Pressing her hands together in her lap, Sam battled an urge to plead with Chilton. After what seemed an eternity, the pounding behind her ears receded and she mastered the trembling in her fingers. Pride stiffened her spine. "Well," she said as graciously as she could manage, "I guess that's it." The smile curving her full lips felt nailed in place. "If things don't work out, Mr. Chilton, I hope you'll remember Adams Air. We'd be happy to have your business again."

Bill Chilton cast her a relieved smile. "You're

being a good sport about this, Miss Adams. Frank would be proud." He looked at them both. "Times are tough. A man has to save a penny if he can."

"I understand," Sam murmured. She understood she'd been bested in a low, underhanded manner. She understood she'd lost another account. The thought of telling her father what had happened made her cringe inwardly; she so badly wanted him to be proud of her. Instead, she was slowly losing everything Frank Adams had worked a lifetime to build.

And she was losing to a man who made her pulses pound when she looked at him.

Chapter Two

What Sam wanted most was to be left alone. She needed another cup of coffee and time to nurse her wounds, time to shore up her battered self-confidence.

Automatically, she murmured polite good-byes, then sank to her chair and stared into her cup. She winced at the thought of letting her father down again, dreaded admitting the outcome of this meeting. The truth was, filling Frank Adams' shoes was proving more difficult than either of them had suspected.

Sighing, Sam tilted her head backward and stared at the ivy spilling from a hanging pot. It wasn't easy being the son Frank Adams hadn't had. Sometimes—not often, but sometimes—she wished she could just walk away from Adams Air. And do what? She didn't know. All of her life she'd been groomed to take over Adams Air when her father retired.

"Sorry about that, darlin', but I need the business worse than you do."

Instantly Sam's thoughts returned to the present. She scowled as Luke Bannister slid into his chair and signaled the waitress for more coffee.

"How do you know what I need?" she asked sharply. Silently she commanded herself to rise and leave, but she suspected her knees wouldn't support her. "The Chilton account was important."

"Adams Air Freight is well established. You've been around a long time. Surely one account isn't going to make or break you." Bannister smiled engagingly. "But it will make or break me."

"You don't know anything about Adams Air!"

He studied her, his eyes becoming serious. "Tell me about it."

Sam bit off the anxious words bubbling to her lips. "Look—you won. You can quit now." She passed a weary hand over her eyes, then shoved a wave of dark curls behind her ear. Why was she sitting here like a lump? She had less than an hour to rush out to the airport and catch her flight home. If the plane arrived in Denver on schedule, she'd have time to drive to the office, total her accounts, and discover how badly Chilton's loss would hurt.

Instead of jumping up, she watched with dull eyes as the waitress refilled their cups. If she was honest with herself, and she usually was, then she had to admit that she didn't want to know the total of her diminishing accounts. Not today.

The shock of Bannister's large, warm hand covering hers jolted her. His thumb stroked the back of her hand and a tingle shot up her arm.

"Sam, darlin', I understand that you're hesitant to believe me when I say I intend to marry you. It has to sound like something a man whispers in a bar to a lady he wants to marry for the night." His fingers tightened around her hand and his blue eyes lifted to hers. "But I mean every word. You're everything I've ever wanted in a woman—beautiful, intelligent, feisty . . ."

Anger blazed in Sam's brown eyes. Anger directed toward Bill Chilton, toward the freight business, toward the world in general and Luke Bannister in particular. Anger was easier to deal with than the heat curling in her stomach at Bannister's touch. She jerked her hand away.

"Knock it off, Bannister. You don't even know

me." Accusation flashed between her lashes. "But you know how to play dirty, don't you! That business about undercutting my price was nasty."

He grinned. "You're right. Want to know how you should have countered?"

"You're damned right I do!"

"You should have undercut my offer by another ten percent."

Sam stared. "What good would that have done? Then you would have undercut again. You would have, wouldn't you?"

A dark lock of hair fell across his forehead as he nodded. "Right. At that point you should have given up and let me have the client. But not before."

"I lose either way. You steal my client." Sam's brow furrowed and her gaze sharpened. She added slowly, "But at a thirty percent reduction in fare."

"And you'd win in the long run."

A reluctant smile spread across her lips. "You couldn't stay in business long with that kind of rate-cutting."

"Exactly."

Sam regarded him silently, fighting to overcome the impression that Clark Gable was staring hungrily at her lips. Luke Bannister, she decided, wasn't at all what she had expected. She still guessed he ran his business in a slapdash manner; her opinion hadn't changed in that area. But she conceded he possessed an unexpected warmth and charm.

"Why are you telling me this?" she asked curiously. Who in his right mind told the competition how to win? Sam would never have done such a thing.

He shrugged. "I like a fair fight, darlin', and this wasn't fair. I had the advantage." A smile lifted the corners of his lips. "You're prettier than me, but I have the pilot stories. The stories will win out every time."

"Don't I know it!" Chilton wasn't the first client she'd lost to Bannister's collection of flying tales, and Chilton probably wouldn't be the last. But at least she could fight him on the rate structure.

Standing, Sam extended a cool hand. "It's getting late, and I have a plane to catch. It's been . . . interesting . . . meeting you."

Bannister enfolded her hand within a hard, callused warmth. "It's not going to be that easy, darlin'. I didn't find you to let you go without a struggle."

He drew her hand against his broad chest, pulling her near enough to feel the heat of his body mingling with the heat of her own. A surprised gasp escaped her lips as she felt her willpower melt away. Her eyes settled on the firm curve of his lips, a tremor swept from her toes to her fingertips. And when she raised her head to meet his intent gaze, her mouth suddenly went dry and her knees threatened to collapse.

What's happening to me, she asked herself frantically. Not even Brad Jennings, the man she'd almost married, had exerted such a disturbing effect on her. Stepping backward, she hastily wrenched herself from Bannister's grasp and nervously smoothed damp palms down across her slacks, realizing too late that her actions called attention to the soft flare of her hips. Quickly, she bent to collect her wool jacket, her purse and her briefcase. The movement brought her watch before her eyes and she uttered a small cry of dismay.

"I've missed my flight! Damn." There was still one more flight to Denver, but it was sold out. She'd checked when she arrived. "I'll have to stand by for the last flight and hope for the best," she muttered, thinking out loud. If the worst happened, she'd stay over and depart in the morning. Her eyes settled on her briefcase, taking a quick inventory of its contents. She'd brought her makeup and a few toiletry items, and an extra sweater.

"You can hitch a ride with me," Bannister offered happily. "I'm ferrying a Fairchild to Denver. We can leave immediately."

Sam studied him uncertainly. The last thing she wanted was to share the next hour with Luke Bannister. On the other hand, what she most wanted was to depart the scene of her defeat, return to her townhouse, and sink into a hot steamy tub.

"It's settled," Bannister said, making up her mind for her. He lifted her briefcase and smiled down at her. "I hope you're noticing that I'm the kind of guy who rescues maidens in distress. You won't be sorry that you married me."

"Now, look here, Bannister . . ." Sam began. Then she looked into his grin and gave up. Moodily she followed him toward the parking lot beyond the mall. They agreed to meet at the freight hangers on the far side of Sardy Field. Already Sam regretted the situation.

Before Bannister swung into his jeep, he leaned over to the window of her rented Toyota. "By the way, darlin', that remark about my company being run like a lemonade stand stabbed me to the heart. I am mortally wounded." Clutching his chest and rolling his eyes toward heaven, Bannister staggered across the lot toward his jeep.

Sam smiled despite herself, then shoved the key into the ignition. She cursed beneath her breath. Luke Bannister had stolen an account from beneath her nose and insulted her by handing her a very old line. So why was she smiling and tingling all over like a schoolgirl in the throes of a serious crush?

Sighing, she pushed a hand through her shoulder-length hair and remembered her father's advice: "There's no disgrace in making a mistake, Sam. The error lies in making the same mistake twice."

It had been a mistake to allow Bannister at her meeting with Chilton. And she had an uneasy feeling that she had compounded the error by accepting a seat on his plane. She watched as Bannister gave her a jaunty salute, then turned the jeep out of the parking lot. Late afternoon sunshine shimmered along the silver at his temples.

Yes, she had a distinct impression that she'd made a serious error. One she would live to regret.

Chapter Three

Sam returned her rental car then hitched a ride on a baggage cart to the freight hangars. When she saw Bannister inspecting the underside of the plane's wings, her spirits sank.

"Is that Bannister's plane?" she blurted to the cart driver. Shading her eyes, Sam stared at the battered Fairchild, noting flaking paint even at a distance. The airplane had logged a lot of miles and all of them showed. "Will that piece of tin fly?" she whispered.

The man driving the baggage cart laughed. "Honey, Luke Bannister can fly anything,"

"I hope you're right," Sam muttered. Reluctantly, she climbed from the cart and slowly approached the Fairchild.

Bannister was kicking tires and scribbling notations on a clipboard. When he saw her, he waved toward an aluminum ladder leading upward into the plane. "High Hopes is leaving in fifteen minutes."

"High Hopes?" Sam grimaced. Why pilots insisted on naming planes as if they were pets bewildered her. Each plane was numbered; that should be enough. She looked at the dark opening above her and frowned uncertainly.

"Hey, Bannister!" A man in greasy coveralls cupped his hands around his mouth and shouted. "You going to get that tub out of here or shall we plant a few trees and landscape it for you?"

"We're leaving now," Luke Bannister laughed. "Up you go, darlin'."

"Wait a minute." Sam chewed her lip and swallowed a rush of panic. "Have you flown this plane before?"

Bannister touched her elbow reassuringly. "Nope. Just bought it. I'm taking it to Denver to be overhauled and put back into shape." Gently but firmly, he took her briefcase from her fingers and guided her up the first rung of the ladder.

"Oh God," Sam groaned.

Then Bannister's hand slid to her waist and covered the small of her back. The unexpected slide of warmth paralyzed her. The possessive strength of his fingers against her sweater shot a tingling shiver through her body and she halted on the step, drawing a long deep breath before she turned, a blaze of warning in her brown eyes. "One thing we need to get straight right now, Bannister—I'm here because I'm in a hurry to get home and because I hope we can arrive at a business truce. That's all."

Her response to his touch had been both surprising and confusing. But she'd made up her mind to ignore it. She had no intention of falling under the spell of his Clark Gable virility. They were adversaries, and she meant to remember that fact.

Pulling sharply from his hand, she hurried up the ladder rungs, grinding her teeth at his low chuckle. Without looking back, she knew he was watching the sway of her hips.

Annoyed, Sam stepped into the Fairchild and paused to allow her eyes a moment to adjust to the dim interior. The Fairchild's passenger seats had been removed and the cabin refitted for cargo. At the moment the hold was empty, except for lengths of nylon webbing and a stack of lumpy tarpaulin.

"You'll ride up front with me," Bannister said, his voice deep near her ear. He tossed her briefcase into the small luggage compartment directly behind the cockpit and strapped it down, then he turned to her, his strong fingers slipping from her shoulder to her back, guiding her forward.

His touch continued to unnerve Sam in a manner she didn't fully understand. Or perhaps she did. A small sound caught in her throat, more a gasp than a protest, and a rush of heat warmed her cheeks. She should have slapped his hand away. But adding to her confusion was an inexplicable conviction that Bannister's touch was right, so perfectly right that she did nothing except lift her wide, puzzled eyes toward his.

Silently she commanded herself to step away, but her body refused to respond. The moment stretched into a disturbing timelessness as she stood immobile, staring into Bannister's steady gaze, watching a flicker of desire flame and grow. The sudden tension in her stomach warned that she should pull away from his hand. But she couldn't move. Not even when his fingers slipped up her arm and gently stroked her cheek.

"I thought I'd never find you," Bannister whispered, his eyes caressing her face, tracing the contours of her lips.

"Please . . ." Sam swayed and swallowed hard. This wasn't like her, she thought frantically. Sam Adams wasn't the type of woman to surrender to sudden violent physical urges. She must be coming down with something—a cold, the flu, a fever.

Wrenching from his hand, she bolted forward and flung herself into the right-hand seat, hiding her confusion by bending over her seat belt. She castigated herself beneath her breath for being a fool. Why in the name of heaven had she allowed him to stroke her cheek? What was the matter with her? She hated the way she was behaving—the blushes, the shaking fingers. Embarrassment heightened the color in her cheeks.

With an effort, Sam steadied her hands against

her purse and collected her thoughts. All right, Bannister wasn't what she'd expected. Wasn't she flexible enough to adjust? Of course she was. She could endure anything and anyone for an hour. Once they landed, she'd never see him again.

Instead of watching as Bannister flicked switches and spun dials, Sam turned to the window and focused on the man in greasy coveralls. At least he didn't release a flutter of butterflies into her stomach.

A vibration began under her feet and the plane rattled to life. Spurts of dark smoke coughed from the engines as their whine heightened into a roar. The man in the coveralls disappeared beneath the plane to remove the chocks, then guided the Fairchild in a semicircle and onto the pad.

Bannister smiled and gave the man a thumb's-up sign, then he rolled the Fairchild along a taxiway toward the single runway.

"Ah—aren't there usually two pilots?" Sam asked, knowing full well the answer. Her tone emerged cool, but her thoughts were not.

"Right. But our copilot showed up too drunk to walk let alone fly. I fired him and sent him home."

"Oh." Pressing her lips together, Sam reminded herself of what both Chilton and the baggage man had claimed. She hoped their assessment of Bannister's ability was correct.

Leaning backward, Sam tried to relax. But relaxation became impossible when her gaze swept the instrument panel. Half a dozen dials and gauges were covered by strips of tape over which someone had scrawled "Inoperative." for the first time, she noticed the lengths of tape holding together the leather seats she and Bannister occupied. She could see flakes of paint peeling from the plane's nose, and she recalled the disturbing burst of oily smoke when

Bannister had fired up the engines. Sam swallowed hard.

"Bannister?"

"Call me darlin' or honey or Luke."

Sam clasped the edges of her purse tightly between her fingers, her wide eyes fixed on the instrument panel. "All that tape—do we need any of those 'inoperative' functions? Is this thing safe?" If any of her pilots had taken out a plane with this many inoperative switches, she would have considered him suicidal and dismissed him immediately.

"As safe as your mother's arms, darlin'. Is your mother alive, by the way?"

"Yes." Sam cast a longing glance toward the terminal, wishing she'd taken her chances with standby.

"Everyone knows Frank Adams. You took over the company when he retired, right?" Bannister fitted the headset loosely over his head, sliding forward one of the earphones so he could hear her reply.

"Yes." Sam arched her neck, staring at the terminal until she could no longer see the tower.

Bannister heaved an exaggerated sigh. "In-laws. I was hoping you were an orphan, but that's all right. I'm sure I'll learn to love your parents. Any brothers or sisters?"

"No." Finally Sam registered what he was saying. Her shoulders stiffened and she glared at him. "Don't you think your little joke has gone far enough? It's not funny anymore."

"That's because I'm not joking."

Bannister swung the Fairchild onto the runway and held it in place as he revved up the engines until the plane vibrated and shook like a racehorse straining at the gate.

Before he released the plane, he turned and stared at her, all hints of amusement vanished from his steady blue eyes.

"I'm going to marry you."

The plane leaped forward, the sudden rush pressing Sam into the taped leather at her back. Her fingers whitened on the arms of the seat and she stared at the ribbon of gray-black tarmac hurtling past the side window. The nose pulled up and suddenly she was blinking at acres of late afternoon sky as clear and deeply blue as . . . as Luke Bannister's eyes, she thought wildly.

Turning away from the sight, she gazed at Bannister's grin of pure happiness, saw the joy of flight in his confident jaw and in the sure steady movement of his large hands.

Sam's lashes squeezed shut, sweeping her cheekbones. She'd put herself in the hands of a madman who was piloting an ancient plane held together by tape and good luck. She, who had always considered herself a rational intelligent being. Her eyes blinked open and she stared straight ahead.

Sardy Field sat in a narrow valley surrounded by steep mountainous ridges; the one-way airstrip allowed no margin for error. Sam held her breath as the Fairchild dipped then soared upward, winding through the mountain canyons, following the river valley below.

Bannister was good, she conceded thankfully. He was very good.

Once the plane leveled, Bannister swiveled to smile at her. But Sam noticed he didn't relax. His gaze continually swept the mountainous terrain slipping past below. Her heart nosedived.

"Are we on VFR or IFR?" Her nerves would explode if she learned he was flying on visual instead of by instrument flight rules. But she had to know.

"Visual."

"Dammit!" Her eyes flared wide and she groaned. "And I'll bet my whole book of business that you're one of those hotshot pilots who can't be bothered to file a flight plan, right?"

"For a ferry flight?" Bannister grinned. "Paperwork will prove the ruination of the civilized world, mark my words. Besides, I'll bet your pilots don't file for a ferry flight either. No one does."

"Bannister, you idiot!" Shock bled the color from Sam's face. Her hands lifted and fell and immediately clutched at the seat arms. "I don't care if this is an empty plane, by God you should always file a flight plan! My pilots do."

"I'll bet *my* book of business that they don't. Not for a ferry." Bannister glanced at her fingers curling over the seat arms, then he peered at her pale cheeks and his eyebrow rose. "Darlin', are you afraid of flying?"

"There are things I'd rather do," Sam admitted through clenched teeth. She pulled her eyes from the horrifying "inoperative" tapes and gazed down at a blur of golden autumn aspens glittering among the pines. "Like eat nails or visit the dentist." Watching the ground was worse than looking at the dials and gauges.

For perhaps the hundredth time, Sam frantically asked herself what she was doing in the air freight business. Safely behind her desk, the business seemed lucrative and reasonable. Aloft, the air freight business became sheer folly, a flirtation with fate. Feeling tiny pearls of perspiration appear on her brow, she shifted in the seat to face Bannister, steadfastly training her eyes on his and nowhere near the dials or the ground.

Bannister stared in disbelief. "There's nothing to be afraid of, darlin'." His strong, bronzed hands gestured broadly. "Up here we're free as a bird. Don't you feel it?" He frowned into Sam's unblinking stare. "We're free of artificial limits." When she remained stonily unconvinced, he clasped the wheel and nodded to himself.

Abruptly, he tilted the plane on its wing and the Fairchild shuddered then leaned into a wide, graceful turn, pivoting on the wing tip. His face lit, filled with pride and a joy Sam couldn't begin to understand.

In horror, she looked down, swearing she could identify each individual leaf rustling on the aspens below. Her stomach rolled in a slow loop and her fingers dug into the leather beneath her nails. Gasping, she cried out, begging him to pull up.

"You're serious, aren't you?"

"I'm about to be serious all over your lap," Sam wheezed, pressing a shaky hand to her stomach. War pilots could no more resist theatrics than they could resist naming their planes. Her father had soured her forever on loops and sharp turns when Sam was a child. She closed her eyes and wiped her pale forehead. And as always, she swore that if she ever placed her feet safely on solid ground, nothing on God's green earth would again entice her to fly. When her lashes fluttered open, Bannister was frowning thoughtfully.

"This could be a problem." He studied her chalky face.

"Luke Bannister, if you don't stop that nonsense, I'm going to scream."

He smiled. "Luke—we're making progress." His smile folded into a frown. "Somehow I always assumed you would love flying like I do."

"You always assumed?" Sam stared at him incredulously. The man heard only what he wanted to hear. She pulled upright in the seat. "Look. You are making me crazy with this." Patience, she told herself, have patience. "How can you possibly assume anything about me? We're strangers!"

Bannister patted her arm, brushing aside her pro-

test. "Not strangers, darlin', at least not for long."
Those blue, blue eyes held her gaze, and Sam felt
herself growing hot and uncomfortable as she
unwillingly responded to the depth of intimacy in his
stare. "I feel as if I've known you always."

Sam felt the same. Only in her case, the reason
was because she'd spent several weeks gnashing her
teeth and pacing her small office and cursing Luke
Bannister. She'd scarcely thought of anyone else
since taking over Adams Air.

Hastily changing the subject, she leaned away
from his hand and caught her lip between her teeth.
"This plane sounds peculiar." She wanted to divert
the conversation, but the plane really did sound
especially noisy. Though, in fairness, she conceded
that she'd never ridden in a plane that sounded as
safe as she thought it should.

Bannister's shoulders and thighs tensed as he
cocked his head to listen. "Sounds fine to me." This
time he patted her knee. "Relax. I'll tell you if there's
anything to worry about."

Sam swung her knee out of reach. "Oh good," she
answered between her teeth. "I feel so much better."

"You should," Bannister laughed. "I'm the best
pilot in the Rocky Mountain region." His gaze swept
the curves of her tense body. "And now that I've
found you, I'm not going to lose you. No risks today."

"Modesty doesn't appear to be one of your better
qualities."

Bannister shrugged, the movement flexing his
broad shoulders. "Confidence is one of the traits you're
going to love about me. And there's a lot more."

Sam shook her head. Did a man like Luke Bannister truly need a phony line of chatter? Remembering
the glances of the women in the restaurant, she
doubted it. So why did he persist?

"Want some coffee?" Bannister unscrewed a thermos and tipped a cloud of steam into the lid.

"Not right now." Squinting, Sam examined him, while hoping she didn't appear to be. Very much against her will, she admired the crinkles fanning out from his eyes, then dropped her gaze to his wide mouth as he slipped on his dark glasses. The lines framing his lips hinted at generous doses of laughter and command.

Bannister sipped from the thermos lid and smiled. "Now then, darlin', tell me all about yourself." His smile widened into a grin. "In case our children ask some day."

Sam threw up her hands in resignation. "You just won't quit."

"I never give up," he admitted cheerfully.

She looked at him and sighed. "Why don't we discuss business instead?"

"I really think we should get acquainted before the wedding."

Sam pushed a hand through her hair. He was wearing her down. "Why don't you tell me about Luke Bannister first?"

"I was born and raised in Durango," he answered promptly. "You'll love my parents and they will adore you. I have a sister that I wouldn't give two cents for and three brothers who are all cattle ranchers. I graduated from the University of Colorado, then went to Vietnam." He poured more coffee, his face expressionless for a moment.

"And . . . ?" She expected him to expand on Vietnam, but he didn't.

"The only important thing you should know is that I was married once for about two weeks." A sheepish grin tugged his lips. "A long time ago when I was twenty and foolish. I went to Las Vegas for the week-

end, and I woke up one morning and this woman
was . . ."

"I don't want to hear this, Bannister."

"Jealousy? That's an encouraging sign."

Sam passed a hand over her eyes. "You're relentless."

"Financially, we're going to be a little strapped at
first unless you're filthy rich. But Bannister Air is
growing and the future is promising."

"Because you're stealing all my accounts."

"Sour grapes, Sam, not worthy of you. They'll be
our accounts when we're married. At the moment
most of what I own is tied up in my planes. But as
soon as they're paid for, we'll have as much money as
you can spend. Okay?"

Sam's mutter was drowned by the peculiar drone
of the engines. She looked at Bannister and shook
her head with an exasperated smile. His lean body
rocked easily with the increasing pitch of the plane,
unlike her own, which pressed tensely into the seat.
It was impossible to relax. The plane quivered
beneath her feet, and the engines positively did not
sound reassuring. Sam leaned to the window, her
smile fading to an anxious frown. The weather was
changing rapidly, threatening one of the quick,
violent storms the Rockies were famous for . . . the
type of sudden storm that had littered the valleys
with broken planes.

"We'll make a hell of a team, darlin'. You supervise the office and all the paperwork that drives a
man crazy, and I'll fly and manage our pilots."

Wisps of low, gray clouds streamed alongside the
windows. Sam's stomach tightened nervously. She
drew her seat belt hard across the front of her wool
slacks and released a low breath, trying not to think
of the jagged mountains looming on either side of the
Fairchild. "Are we losing altitude or am I imag-
inging it?"

After draining the last of his coffee, Bannister smiled. "I told you, Sam, darlin', when it's time to worry, I'll tell you."

Whether to reassure her or because the clouds had thickened, Bannister indulged her by shifting in his seat and staring into the swirling grayness flowing around them.

Handing Sam the thermos lid, he asked her to replace it. "Could get a little rough," he added casually. "But nothing an ace pilot can't handle. Sit tight, we'll be above this in a few minutes."

When Sam heard his quick intake of breath, she straightened abruptly from the thermos and glanced quickly out the side window. The thermos slipped from her suddenly nerveless fingers. Through a thin break in the clouds, she stared directly into the side of a mountain. "Oh, my God!" she whispered hoarsely.

Bannister's thick brows drew together. A heavy frown pleated his cheeks into deep creases. Cool, clear eyes rapidly scanned the instrument panel. "Something's wrong," he muttered. "We aren't climbing."

The Fairchild shuddered from nose to tail section, straining against buffeting gusts of strong wind. The plane's violent rise and fall threw Sam's heart into her throat, then flung it toward her knees. Gripping the seat arms until her fingers ached, she turned wide, frightened eyes on Bannister.

A thin, dark wisp of smoke curled from the instrument panel.

Bannister glanced briefly at the pungent drift, then leaned forward, squinting to pierce the thickness of clouds against the window. His large hands fought the wheel. "Darlin', I think it's time to worry just a little."

Sam nodded and stared straight ahead, her eyes huge and dark in her white face.

Chapter Four

Sam's pulse thundered in her ears, drowning the terrifying cough and sputter of the engines. The acrid smell of burning electrical wire stung her nostrils. She stared at the instrument panel and her heart lurched as flashing red lights lit up the cockpit. Resolutely, she turned a chalky face to the window, blinking rapidly as the clouds parted intermittently to reveal the terrain.

A strangling gulp of hot air lodged in her throat, and instinctively she threw out a hand, gripping Bannister's tense forearm. He shrugged off her hand as the wind flung the plane hard to the right. Sam watched blindly as the stones and boulders littering the mountain loomed suddenly from the mist, not twenty feet away.

They were going to crash.

"Brace!" Bannister shouted.

One moment the right wing was attached to the plane, the next instant it was gone. A deafening ripping sound sliced through Sam's consciousness, then the roar of rushing air. Whipping her head to the side, she stared wide-eyed past the cockpit door and down the length of the hold.

The tail section had vanished, severed by the pinwheeling wing. Sam stared out at sky and mountain ridge.

Amazingly, they remained airborne. But not for long. The left wing dropped, its unbalanced weight pulling them down into a long, sickening slide; they were falling toward a grassy valley far below. The plane tilted crazily and Sam hung in her seat, suspended by the belt, her hair swinging past her wild eyes.

"It is definitely time to worry," Bannister muttered between his teeth. His hands flew over the switches, battled the wheel. And he rode the plane down under the boiling clouds, fighting to hold the remaining wing steady, struggling to control the slant and rate of descent.

Sam's teeth ground together so violently that her jaw hurt. A bell was shrieking over her head, but she didn't hear it any more than she heard the savage hammering of her heart. During the seconds remaining before impact, she thought of everything and nothing. Strange disconnected memories flashed through her mind—brief joys, sorrows which were no longer important, regrets. Many regrets. She hadn't truly loved or been loved, she would never bear children . . .

The ground rushed upward with horrifying speed.

Bannister watched with a stony expression, squinting against the smoke building in the cockpit. "Now!" he shouted and leaned hard on the wheel.

The flaps extended along the wing and abruptly the wing soared upward and suddenly all Sam could see was gray sky. Her body wrenched violently to the right, crushing against the bulkhead, and she screamed as the plane crashed into the meadow, hurtling forward. Cheek flat against the window, she watched rocks and grass flying past directly beneath her terrified eyes.

She whispered a silent prayer that the end would be swift, that neither of them would suffer a lingering death.

"Hang on," Bannister shouted. "The wing is coming down!"

Metal screamed against stone. Rocks tore at the landing gear. As the wheels collapsed, the broken tail descended, then the wing.

A shower of sparks exploded outward as the wing tip dug into the earth, spinning the fuselage in a sudden, violent arc. For an instant the world whirled crazily before Sam's wild eyes, then finally the mutilated Fairchild shuddered to a halt.

Sam held her breath in frozen silence, staring blindly at the heavy haze of dust and dirt swirling against the cracked windows. Bannister crossed his arms on the wheel and dropped his forehead against them, breathing deeply.

Seconds before Bannister spoke, Sam became aware that he had slipped to her side. She didn't respond when his hard, warm hand cupped her shoulder.

"Darlin'? Are you hurt? Talk to me."

Incredulously, she turned from the settling dust, her dark stare wide and blank. "We're alive," she whispered, her voice cracking. "Alive!"

"Listen to me, Sam." Blue eyes stared intently into hers. "Raise your knees to your chest. Can you do that? Raise your knees to your chest."

Silently, she did as he commanded, her eyes not leaving his.

"Good. Now both your arms. Raise them above your head."

Her left arm moved easily; her right arm ached so badly the effort to lift it raised a groan to her lips. But the pain resulted from the battering bruising she had endured; nothing was broken.

"Look at me," Bannister ordered.

Responding like an automaton, Sam turned to face him. Shock had drained the color from her cheeks, her pulse continued to pound so loudly she knew he must hear it.

Bannister frowned. "That's a bad cut. Here." He jerked a snowy handkerchief from his jeans and wiped her temple, then pressed the handkerchief into her shaking hand. "Press hard until it stops bleeding."

Bleeding? Sam blinked at the red smear staining his handkerchief then raised trembling fingers to her hair. She stared at the wetness on her fingers in disbelief. She felt nothing.

Bannister's hand closed around her cold fingers and raised them to her head. "Press hard."

She wet her lips and tried to speak. No sound emerged. She tried again. "Luke . . . will the plane blow up?"

"If there's no fire now, there isn't going to be any," he soothed, brushing the hair from her cheek. "We're all right." He peered into her eyes, then held up his hand. "How many fingers?"

"Three," Sam answered promptly. Gradually, her faculties returned as she began to grasp that the terror had ended. They were alive. Miraculously alive. She was bruised all over, but she was alive.

Anxiously, she clasped his wrist, drawing comfort from the strong, steady pulse beneath her fingers. "Are you all right?"

Bannister's smile was grim. "My pride is fatally damaged. But the rest of me seems okay."

Sam examined him rapidly as her vision sharpened and her mind cleared. He was as battered and bruised as she but moving freely, nothing broken. He was going to have a beauty of a black eye, though.

Without warning a sudden powerful sense of urgency overwhelmed her. She had to escape, had to leave the airplane. Now. She couldn't breathe; she felt the walls crushing in around her. She had to stand on firm earth and test her arms and legs her-

self and fall on her shaking knees and thank God
they had survived. And she had to do it now.

When her frantic fingers stumbled over the seat
belt, Bannister gently snapped the latch, freeing
her. Sam rose on rubbery legs, leaning slightly backward against the steep downward tilt of the floor.
Wincing, she touched the ache across her stomach
where the belt had bitten into her flesh.

"Okay?" Bannister steadied her, clasping her
elbows.

Still pressing the handkerchief above her ear, Sam
nodded and rested briefly against his chest. Then she
turned sideways and slowly descended the slant,
moving toward the jagged open end where the tail
section had been.

"Wait." Bannister jumped down and lifted his
arms to her, easing her to the ground.

Silently, they waded through knee-high grass
toward a granite boulder, then leaned against it.
Sam closed her eyes and gloried in the sensation of
stone and heat. Minutes ago she hadn't expected to
feel anything ever again.

When she opened her eyes, Bannister had stepped
forward a few paces and was standing, hands on
hips, staring at the plane in grim silence.

Reluctantly Sam forced herself to follow his gaze.
Her heart froze in her chest. The nose of the broken
Fairchild pointed toward heaven; the sheered end of
the fuselage rested on the meadow floor. The silvery
wing tip was buried in a mound of dark earth.

No one should have survived. It was a miracle they
were alive. Sam swallowed hard, her mouth suddenly dry. A violent tremble began in her toes and
swept upward, enveloping her body in waves of ice.
Her teeth chattered uncontrollably as she listened to
the awful dusty silence. Hoarsely, she whispered his
name. "Luke?"

Bannister examined her white face and shivering body then opened his arms. "Come here, darlin'," he said quietly.

She ran to him, burrowing deeply into the solid warmth of his arms, her body shaking like a slender reed in a gale. A babble of words poured against the hollow of his throat, a torrent of broken phrases moist with the threat of tears.

He pressed her head to his shoulder. "Shhh. It's safe now. It's all right."

"I saw the rocks and trees and I knew we would crash. I thought we were going to die, and I . . ."

"It's over now, we're all right. You're safe, darlin'."

She clung to his strength and warmth, to the low rumble of his voice in her ear. When he moved to shrug out of his jacket, she cried out in protest, needing the comfort of his solid, hard body, needing him as she'd never needed anything in her life.

"Samantha, darlin', take my jacket."

"I thought . . ."

"Shhh." When she wouldn't allow him to remove the jacket, he wrapped her tightly in his arms, gently kissing her hair, her wounded temple.

Sam's shaking fingers dug into his shoulders and her head fell backward as his quiet kisses slowly soothed her wildly shuddering body.

"Hold me, just hold me." Trembling against him, she rested in his strong arms, feeling his lips tender yet firm against her eyelids as he kissed away her tears. Seeking his warmth and safety, she pressed hard against his body, unable to get close enough, even though his arms tightened around her, molding her to his chest and thighs. It wasn't enough. She wanted to melt into him, to become part of his solid strength and confidence.

The handkerchief fluttered from her head, but she made no effort to retrieve it, afraid to break the bond between them, unwilling to abandon the slow, steady warmth flowing back into her limbs.

His large hands slid along the curve of her back, caressing her, gentling her like a frightened animal. And his wide mouth trailed soft kisses across her forehead, her temples, her trembling eyelids.

"Luke . . ." Sam opened her eyes and caught her breath at the intensity in his steady gaze. "Oh, Luke . . ."

"We're safe," he murmured, his mouth brushing the corner of her parted lips. "We're safe now."

She stared into his eyes, which were not blue now but dark with the growing desire aroused by her full breasts crushing against his chest, by the pressure of her hips and pelvis molded tightly to his.

"Luke . . ."

"Shhh."

Her hands lifted and shaking fingers explored his face in wonder as she reassured herself that he was real. She could prove her own survival only by being certain of his. Cautiously she touched the silvery strands threading his temples, dropped her hands to frame his tanned cheeks. And her eyes moved over his strong, angular face, from the thickness of his dark lashes to the sensual curve of his mouth so near her own that she felt his warm breath on her lips.

He held her and stared into her wide eyes, understanding. Then he gently kissed her, his mouth soft and reassuring. A sob caught in Sam's throat as she surrendered to the quiet pressure of his lips. Her arms circled his neck, her fingers buried in the tousled black curls above his collar, and she clung to his body and to his mouth and to the solid reality of life, of feeling, of tingling, heated sensation.

"Sam. My beautiful Sam."

Bannister's hands slid from her spine to the curve of her hips, and he guided her against his body until she felt the tensing of his hard thighs, felt the unmistakable swell of his desire as his mouth covered hers in a kiss that was no longer gentle, but a demanding reaffirmation of glorious life. Sam parted her lips beneath his kiss and darted her tongue forward, each electric sensation more vivid and concentrated than ever before in her life.

They had almost died; but they had survived. Sam's nerves quivered on the surface of her skin, more alive than she could ever remember. She craved the proof of sensation, of glorious feeling. She reveled in the unexpected blessing of touch and sight and smell and raw, vivid emotion.

Frantic to satisfy her need for life, she drew away from his lips, her breath hot in her throat, and she touched the triangle of crisp, dark hair at Luke's collar. Closing her eyes, she opened her senses to the full wondrous impact of touch and texture. And when Luke's hand slipped upward beneath her sweater to stroke the silky skin on her back, she understood his need was as great as her own.

Lips clinging, they explored each other, discovering as if for the first time the satiny smoothness of firm skin, the silky texture of hair, the scent and taste of growing desire.

And a wonderful flow of heat raced along Sam's flaming body, thawing the numbing chill of fear. She gazed into the intense blue of Luke's stare and felt the joy of color, of actually experiencing blue, of knowing it and realizing it and feeling it deep inside.

Cupping his face between her palms, she gazed deeply into his eyes, an expression of wonderment stealing over her features. "I never understood blue before," she said, marveling. A wild happiness swept her body and she couldn't stand still. They were alive! She flung out her arms and joy illuminated her face. "We're alive!" Throwing her arms around his neck, she hugged him until he grinned, then she spun away and shouted to the sky, "We are alive!"

He caught her at the end of her spin and held her for a moment, his lips brushing her hair. Then he laced his fingers into hers and together they turned to look at the plane.

Gradually Sam's smile faded and her joy evaporated. Uneasily she glanced at the rugged mountains towering above them, noting the first hints of sunset pinking the edges of the clouds. Soon it would be dark.

There was more to survival than living through the crash. Wetting her lips, Sam glanced at Luke Bannister and quietly withdrew her hand from his. "What do we do now?"

Chapter Five

❧

"Well, as it appears we'll be here overnight . . ."

"Overnight?" Sam looked up at him and blinked.

". . . we'll need shelter and a fire."

Biting her lip, Sam frowned at the deepening shadows slanting across the autumn grasses. Of course they'd be here overnight. Rescue attempts couldn't begin until morning. She rubbed her sore arm and ribs then nodded soberly and drew a breath. "What can I do to help?"

"Were you ever a girl scout, darlin'?" Bannister smiled down at her.

"A long time ago."

"Well, see what you can remember about building a fire." Bannister stroked her cheek. "And I'll see about rigging us a place out of the wind."

Thoughtfully, Sam watched him stride toward the plane, wondering what he felt when he looked at the broken Fairchild, his "High Hopes."

She knew the crash wasn't his fault; weather in the Rockies didn't respect pilot expertise. Their survival, on the other hand, she credited entirely to him. Without Bannister's skill, without his sure hands on the wheel, Sam was certain the outcome would have been very different. A light shiver rippled across her shoulders. Instead of dwelling on what might have happened, she forcefully applied her thoughts toward enduring the night as comfortably as possible.

Squaring her shoulders, she marched through the

wild grass toward a stand of pine and golden aspen. After gathering an armload of dead, dry limbs, she carried them to the plane and deposited the wood near the fuselage before returning for more. The night would be long and cold before morning. On the fourth trip, she gathered leaves, autumn crisp and easy to kindle.

"That should hold us." She dusted her hands across her slacks.

Bannister leaned from the body of the plane. "Good. Are you going to dig a fire pit?"

"Of course. Have you got a shovel in there?"

Bannister muttered something she didn't hear, then his dark head reappeared. "Improvise, darlin'," he said patiently. "Improvisation is the key here."

"I know that," Sam answered crisply, her competitive spirit flaring. She bit her tongue, recognizing this was neither the time nor the place for competing. Annoyed with herself, she approached the tail and peered inside. Bannister patiently wielded a small penknife, cutting lengths of tarp.

"I'll use the thermos lid," she decided, pulling herself inside the plane and wincing as her battered muscles protested. The slant was steep enough that she had to grasp the strips of nylon webbing to prevent a slide back to the ground.

"Not a good idea. We're going to need that cup."

Sam's lips pressed into a thin smile. "All right," she said lightly. She didn't like having her ideas countermanded. "I'll work it out." Struggling upward, she pulled herself inside the cockpit and rested her weight against the tilted wall. The wreckage was worse than shock had allowed her to recall.

The full length of the instrument panel was scorched brown; the hot stench of smoldering wire still filled the confined space. Cracks webbed all the windows. Loose paper littered the floor and leather seats, ruffled by the faint breeze entering through the cracks and the open tail.

Sam closed her eyes and shoved a shaking hand through her hair, swallowing hard. Those last terrifying seconds would haunt her nightmares for years to come. But she'd worry about that later. Sweeping a slow gaze about the cockpit, she searched for something suitable for digging. There was nothing.

Retreating, she passed Bannister without a word and emerged into the shadows deepening outside. Eyes to the ground, she followed the rut gouged by the wing tip until she found what she was seeking, a wedge of torn metal. If she wrapped the sharp edges, the metal sliver would provide an adequate tool.

She returned to the cockpit and retrieved the roll of tape she assumed had been used to tape the seats. This time when she descended, she muttered to Bannister, "You should have a fire in a few minutes."

"I knew you'd work it out," he replied genially, sawing the penknife across the tarp. He glanced up as she slipped past him, his eyes sweeping the lush curve of her breasts. "I can't remember—do you have a jacket?"

"Yes."

"You'll need it before morning." After rummaging in his pocket, he produced a lighter. "Here. You'll need this, too."

"Do you smoke?"

"A pipe sometimes."

She could just see it. If Clark Gable hadn't smoked a pipe, he should have. Sighing, Sam eased down the slant and then applied herself to digging the fire pit. She lined it with stones then lit the kindling. In a few minutes, she was warming her hands over a satisfactory glow of flames. So far so good. She'd held up her end.

This time when she poked her head into the

plane's body, her smile was a bit smug. "The fire is crackling. How are you coming on the shelter part?"

He wiped his forehead, then asked her to move aside. He bunched a length of tarp, then dropped it out the end of the plane. "It's coming along."

"Good."

"Darlin'? Do you have any perfume in your brief-case?"

Sam's brow rose in surprise. "I think so. Why?"

"Because I'm finished here, and now I want another look at the cut on your head." After pulling himself up to the luggage rack, he removed her briefcase then followed her outside the plane and gently pushed at the hair matted along the edges of her cut.

"Ouch!"

"That's good. You're feeling it now."

"You're damned right I'm feeling it. What on earth are you doing?"

The warmth of his large body reminded Sam of the strange wild need she'd felt for him earlier. A flush of heat shot upward from her breast. Remembering the strength of his arms, the thrust of his muscled thighs, intensified the color in her cheeks. She frowned and stared at a point above his head. She couldn't imagine how she had behaved so crazily, hurling herself into his arms, almost begging him to hold and kiss her. It was shock, of course. Shock did strange things to people.

Bannister's large hands dropped from her head and he leaned to open her briefcase. "Neatly packed; I like that. You'll be a good housekeeper."

"Are you going to start that again?" A small exas-perated groan accompanied Sam's words.

Arching a black eyebrow, Bannister grinned up at her. "You might as well accept it, Samantha, girl, we're made for each other."

Refusing to respond to his nonsense, Sam leaned down and pushed her fingers beneath sheafs of paper. "Here. Here's what you're looking for."

Bannister examined the bottle. "Chanel number five. I'd better plan on making a lot of money." For a moment his gaze darkened on the plane, then he twisted off the cap of the perfume bottle and stood, motioning Sam to do the same. "Front and center, darlin'."

"What are you going to do?"

"I'm going to disinfect that cut."

She stared. "With perfume?"

"With a mixture that is about eighty percent alcohol if I remember correctly."

"That's about right," Sam conceded slowly. Subdued, she submitted quietly, standing in front of him trying not to look at lips whose kisses had been so incredibly vivid in the wake of the crash. When the perfume splashed across the cut and ran into her hair, she yelped. It hurt like hell.

Bannister grinned. "If it doesn't hurt, it isn't doing any good."

Sam fanned her hand furiously near her hair, her eyes tearing at the fumes. He was so infuriatingly right. Turning from his amusement, she bent to her case and removed her extra sweater, thankful to have it. After thinking a moment, she untied the bright scarf at her throat and knotted it around her head, then pulled on the second sweater.

"Better put your cap on, it's starting to get chilly." The temperature seemed to be dropping by the minute as the sun faded behind the mountains in a burst of dying pink. "You lose more heat from the head than from any other part of the body." Score one for the girl scouts.

Obligingly, Bannister pulled his cap from his hip pocket and tugged it over his black curls. "Okay, darlin', let's take care of the shelter before we lose all the light. Where do you want to sleep?"

"What are the choices?" Sam asked, keeping her tone as businesslike as possible. She hoped he understood the kisses had been nothing more than a natural aftermath of the crash.

"We'll gain the most protection from the wind by sleeping under the tail. The protruding section will provide a ceiling."

Sam considered the jagged edges doubtfully. He was correct, but on the other hand, she worried that the plane might shift and settle. "It doesn't look all that secure to me," she said finally.

"Okay, we'll pitch a tent out here."

Sam's eyebrows soared in surprise. "Just like that? No argument?"

Bannister shrugged. "Darlin', I expect to be rearranging furniture for you the rest of my life. Might as well start now. You tell me where you want the tent and I'll put it there."

"Luke, please." Sam's shoulders dropped and she heaved an exaggerated sigh. "This is wearing thin. I'd appreciate it if you would drop this line. Agreed?"

"I told you, darlin'—I'm serious."

Sam regarded him silently. "Suppose I told you that I don't ever plan to marry? Suppose I told you that I don't have time for men, that my goal is to build Adams Air into the biggest and best air freight company in the west?"

He sighted along a jagged spike protruding from the broken tail section. "I'd tell you that you are crazy, my love. And"—he selected the longest log from the pile of firewood she'd collected—"and I'd tell you that I'll put you out of business if that's what it takes to get your mind on marrying me." He pounded the log into the ground using a rock as a hammer. Between blows he glanced up at Sam's

incredulous stare. "Supper is your job. I think Jack—
that was our drunk copilot—left his lunch box
behind. If so, it's probably in the cockpit."

Sam's mouth dropped open. "You'll put me out of
business?" she repeated in disbelief.

"I thought I noticed some candy in your briefcase."

"Bloody hell you'll put me out of business!" Sparks
flew from her snapping brown eyes. "You aren't that
good, Bannister. I'll put *you* out of business!"

He laughed. "Do it after supper, okay?" His arms
lifted and he gave the log a final pounding. "Remember supper? Your job?"

She turned away from his wide grin and ground
her teeth. When she returned with the lunch box,
still fuming, he had strung a rope from the metal
splinter to the log and was draping a length of tarp
over the rope. Sam fisted her hands on her hips and
considered. It was going to be a small tent, very
small. While Bannister smoothed another tarp over
the ground inside the makeshift tent, Sam poked
through the lunch box, discarding crumpled wrap-
pers into the fire and then unwrapping a sandwich.

"It's peanut butter and jelly," she announced when
he emerged from the tent.

"I love peanut butter and jelly," he said cheerfully.

She simply couldn't imagine it. Even with his eye
beginning to swell and purple, Bannister resembled
Clark Gable to a startling degree. Sam could not
visualize Clark Gable eating a peanut-butter-and-
jelly sandwich. Her lips curved in a lopsided smile as
she tried to picture Gable sauntering into the dining
hall at Tara. "Good evening, Miss Scarlett, make
mine a peanut butter and jelly." Not in a million
years.

"Why are you smiling?"

She grinned up at him. "No reason." No, not in a
million years. Shaking her head, she poked around

in the lunch box, discovering an apple and a small bag of chips. Spirits restored, she opened her briefcase and withdrew her prize, chocolate-covered raisins. "We'll have a feast," she said brightly as he dropped down beside her on a log facing the fire.

Full darkness had fallen across the meadow, and with it came the chill of an autumn night. After buttoning her jacket, Sam laid their dinner on the small squares of tarp he gave her, then warmed her hands before the flames.

"How would you feel about splitting the sandwich and saving the rest for later?" Bannister asked quietly.

"Why?" She studied the shadowed firelight flickering across his strong face. The log they shared was small, and she could feel the brush of his thigh when she moved. Quickly glancing away from eyes too blue and too near, she examined the items at her feet. "Do you really think we need to conserve our food? Surely they'll find us in the morning."

"Maybe."

"Maybe?" Her head snapped up, and she stared at him directly, her breath snagging at his sober gaze. "What do you mean, 'maybe'?" Her thoughts raced then her dark eyes widened in terrible realization. "Luke! You didn't file a flight plan!"

"Darlin' . . . is anyone expecting you in Denver tonight? Someone who might do some checking when you don't show up?" From his tone, Sam knew no one was expecting him.

"No," she whispered hoarsely. When her father didn't hear from her, he'd assume she'd stayed in Aspen for a few days as he'd suggested. Sam blinked at nothing. "I won't be missed for several days," she said slowly.

Silently, Bannister poked a stick at the fire.

"Wait a minute!" Sam clasped his arm, feeling the

tight muscles beneath her fingers. "The ELT! The Emergency Locator Transmitter is sending out signals." Hope shone from her eyes, excited her voice. The ELT activated on impact, pulsing distress signals to passing aircraft. "We had one, didn't we?"

Bannister nodded but he didn't share her excitement. "The ELT was in the tail, Sam. And the tail is somewhere on the other side of that ridge." They both stared at the hulking ebony shadow rising sharply in front of them. Bannister shifted on the log. "Hopefully, it activated—but we can't overlook the possibility that it was crushed on impact. Or fell into the cushion of a pine bough. We can't be certain it's working."

Sam battled the sudden wedge of panic blocking her chest. She studied her hands. There was a simple method of checking the ELT. All Bannister had to do was tune his radio to the emergency frequency. If the ELT was transmitting, the radio would pick up the signal.

"Our radio is smashed, isn't it?" she asked quietly.

"And the compass. And a lot of other items that could have been useful." Suddenly he straightened on the log and clasped her wrist, staring down at her watch. "Keep this wound, darlin', because mine is smashed. As long as your watch is running and accurate, we have a compass."

Sam didn't question, her mind had halted, frozen by the dawning realization that no one would be searching for them. Dropping her head backward, she stared at a sprinkling of bright early stars, unprepared to contemplate the pitifully small supply of food at her feet. "We're in trouble, aren't we, Bannister?" she whispered, her voice strangling.

"Hell no, darlin'. At least not yet." His strong fingers cupped her chin and he turned her firmly to face him. "We have a warm fire and a place to sleep. We have something to eat and, thank God, neither of us is seriously hurt. And . . ."

"If you tell me that we have the stars up above and the earth down below, Bannister, I'm going to slug you." Her eyes narrowed. "And I'll slug you if you say you'll tell me when to worry."

". . . and we have each other. Things could be a lot worse." His eyes lingered on her lips before she wrenched her face away.

Sam pounded her fist against her knee. "Dammit! How could you do such an idiotic thing?" She sprang to her feet and stormed back and forth before the fire. The threat of furious tears sparkled in her eyes. "How could you dare risk these mountains without a flight plan?" She kicked savagely at a log, sending it spinning into the fire pit amid a shower of sparks. She raised a hand to cover her eyes. "My God! Do you realize it could be days before anyone even knows we're missing?"

"The ELT might be working."

"*Might* be!"

Luke Bannister stared into the leaping flames, his face as hard as carved granite. "You're right, Sam," he said finally, his voice proud and stiff. "You're right about everything. It was unforgivably stupid not to file a flight plan."

The fight drained from Sam's heart as she scrutinized his firelit features. She was a fool if she believed he was taking this in stride. For the rest of his life, she suspected Luke Bannister would agonize over what had gone wrong. He would punish himself unmercifully, wondering if he could have done something differently and prevented the crash. She wondered uneasily how long he would flagellate himself before he let it go. If he ever did.

"Look," she said, spreading her hands. "I—I'm sorry. This isn't the time for recriminations. I'm just

. . . I'm just cold and hungry and more than a little scared."

"I know," Bannister answered quietly, looking up at her. "So am I." Pushing to his feet, he reached inside the tail section and withdrew a bottle of Scotch. "I was saving this for dessert, but I think we could use a drink now."

"Bannister—if you had Scotch, why did you pour perfume on my head?" The strong fragrance of Chanel clung about her shoulders in a flowery cloud, choking each breath.

"Because," he smiled tightly as he tipped a generous splash into the thermos lid, "we can't afford to waste this. We can drink Scotch but we can't drink your perfume." He extended the lid.

The fiery liquid burned down Sam's throat, curling warmly in her stomach. "Thank you." She returned the thermos lid and watched as he swallowed deeply, then refilled the cup. Sighing, she sank to the log and settled herself at his side. Silently, they passed the cup and watched the fire crackling against the darkness.

"Are you sore?" he asked.

"All over. You?"

"The same."

A silence fell between them. Sam thought back over the day; the meeting with Bill Chilton seemed light-years away.

"Bannister? Luke?"

"Yes?"

She drew a long breath and stared into the flames. "You were wonderful today. I can't think of another pilot who could have landed that plane. I owe you my life."

"I'll take it," he said promptly. She heard the smile in his tone, then his voice sobered. "You were terrific, too, Sam. No hysterics, no falling apart. We're both lucky."

His arm moved up and circled her shoulders. After a brief hesitation, Sam relaxed and wearily rested her head on his shoulder. The mountain silence beyond the small glow of their fire seemed vast and frighteningly empty. The insignificance of two small humans huddled against the night and the dark forces of nature overwhelmed Sam. Closing her lashes, she turned her face into his neck, drawing on the reassuring touch of another human being to prop up her sinking spirits.

"Luke? We're going to make it, aren't we?" The Scotch had calmed her earlier outburst, and the warm touch of his solid, wide chest beneath her fingertips eased the sense of loneliness banding her chest. Drowsily, she inhaled the clean, honest scent of sweat and man. And Chanel Number Five.

He nestled her head against his shoulder, his thumb softly stroking her cheek. "Darlin', I promise you that I'll get you out of here one way or another."

The stony conviction roughening his tone sent a shiver down Sam's spine, and she tried to raise her head to observe his expression, but he held her firmly against his shoulder.

"I'll get us out," he repeated quietly, his lips moving against the top of her scarf.

Sam nodded and yawned, suddenly exhausted. She felt drained. Her body ached. She gazed longingly at the tent.

Bannister raised her chin. "Sleepy?"

"Uh-huh." Rising, Sam stretched, wincing as her body popped and creaked.

"Blankets are inside." Reading the question darkening her eyes, the flare of unease, Bannister shook his head and smiled. "It's small, darlin', a one-man tent. I'll be right here if you need anything."

Sam's relief released a long, low breath. She met his eyes above the fire. "You know something, Luke Bannister?" she asked softly. "You really are a special man."

A tired smile lifted the corners of his mouth. "That's what I keep tellin you. The day you marry me is going to be the luckiest day of your life." He tossed another log on the fire. "Sleep well, Sam."

Sometime during the night, Sam awoke and crawled to the opening of the tent, peering out in an attempt to identify what had awakened her.

Bannister sat on the cold ground, his spine propped against the log, his head dropped forward on his chest. His arms were folded tightly across his body and he was shivering in his sleep.

Sam stared at him. Luke Bannister had saved her life. And he had given her both the blankets. She sighed and cursed herself for a fool. Then she went to him and shook him awake, leading him silently into the shelter of the tent.

"Sam . . ."

"Shhh. Lie down." The wind and cold had turned his hands to ice.

Shivering at his touch, she tugged his arms around her and she nestled snugly into his trembling body. After covering them with the thin blankets, she spooned herself into the curve of his large frame, offering him her warmth as he had offered his when she had needed comfort.

"Beautiful Sam," he murmured, teeth chattering.

"Go to sleep," she whispered. "It's going to be a long day tomorrow."

After a short time, she felt him relax and his shivering gave way to slow steady breathing. She lay within the shelter of his strong arms, feeling the rise and fall of his chest against her back, fitting into the curve of him as if she had never slept anywhere else.

Sam Adams stared into the blackness and silently attempted to sort out her emotions. Was she falling for him? Falling for the oldest line in the world? For a man who coolly announced he would put her out of business?

Outrageous. But how else could she explain her reaction to him?

His breath flowed warmly across her cheek and she shifted uneasily, acutely aware of his arms enclosing her, of his thighs cupping her buttocks, his long legs tangled with hers. A rush of heat tingled along her body, and she thanked God that he slept.

Thrusting such disturbing thoughts from her mind, Sam nestled her cheek into his opened palm and closed her lashes. Everything would seem simpler in the bright light of day. Like it or not, she couldn't think clearly with his arms around her.

"I'll think about it tomorrow," she murmured, smiling. Then she pressed into his solid warmth and slept.

Chapter Six

"Rise and shine, darlin'."

Sam groaned and opened her eyes as Luke pulled the tarp from the rope over her head. A crisp clean sky arched above, so blue it looked painted in place.

"Do I smell coffee?" She hoped so. Maybe a cup of hot coffee would ease the stiffness from her muscles. Her slender body creaked with the aches and pains from the crash and from sleeping on the ground. She sat up and pulled off her scarf, shaking h r hair free as Luke handed her the thermos lid with a smile.

"It isn't fresh, but it's hot."

"It's terrific." Standing, she tasted the coffee with murmurs of appreciation. He'd pounded a piece of metal into a bowl shape and heated the thermos coffee over the coals. "You've been busy," she observed, then grinned at his black eye. A streak of purple began at the bridge of his nose and swung to the outer corner of his eye.

"I'm an early riser," he answered, ignoring her grin.

Sam watched him fold the tarp and rope it into a square package. Then she carefully stretched and inhaled the brisk mountain air. The fresh, cool scents and the vibrant greens and golds reminded her of a camping trip somewhere in her distant past.

Wandering to the other side of the plane, she sipped her coffee slowly, making it last, and looked around her. While she'd slept, Luke had gathered stones and arranged them in a large arrow. Bending, she inspected a row of items laid out before the fuse-lage. A rough square of metal shaped like a platter, the penknife, the lighter, two piles of nylon webbing, a folded map, the lunch box, tape, and rope.

"What's all this?"

He placed the roped tent beside the other items, then straightened and rubbed his hands against the small of his back. "Tell you over breakfast." Picking up the map, he pushed it into his pocket.

They split the peanut-butter-and-jelly sandwich and finished the coffee, then Sam shifted to face him on the log. "Now, what's this all about?" She had an uneasy suspicion that she already knew.

After lightly touching her cheek, he trickled enough dirt on the fire to make it smoke. The white signal drifted toward the empty sky.

"All right, darlin', here's our situation." Lifting a hand, he pointed upward to a craggy outcrop of rocks. "I found enough water in crevices and natural bowls to almost fill the thermos. But that's it. Once this water is gone, we're going to have to work for more and work hard. We can dig holes and hope for ground seepage—we can collect dew in the morning. You can do a rain dance. Or . . ."

"Or?" She watched him, her sober brown eyes large in her face.

"Or we can walk out of here. Find a stream and fol-low it to civilization."

Sam nodded slowly, staring at her low-heeled shoes. They hadn't been designed for extensive hiking. Neither had she, she decided ruefully.

Luke spread the map at their feet and pointed. "As nearly as I can determine, we're about here." His fin-ger moved across the page. "We're closest to Lead-ville. And there are streams and creeks every few miles. About all we have to do is find one and follow it down."

"All we have to do . . ." Sam wet her lips. Eyes wide, she scanned the mountains enclosing them, bright and sharp-edged in the hard autumn sunlight. His idea overwhelmed her. "You don't think we'll be rescued, then?"

He raised his eyes and she suddenly thought of his large, warm frame wrapped around her during the night. "We might be, Sam, but I'm not sure we can afford to wait. We can do without food, but we can't survive without water. We need to find a water supply. And soon."

"I see."

"May I have your watch?"

Silently, she slid it from her wrist and watched as he improvised a compass, explaining as he did so. By aligning the hour-hand with the sun, south was halfway between the hour-hand and twelve. Bending, he checked the watch against the map. "It won't be an easy hike," he muttered, sitting on his heels and staring at the map. "But it could have been worse. Fortunately, most of the divide is behind us."

Sam leaned to blink at the map, struggling to accept his suggestion. "How far is it to Leadville?"

"I'd say—oh, about thirty or thirty-five miles." He looked at her stricken expression. "A two- or three-day walk. Maybe four."

Over mountains that defeated her just to look at them. Sam swallowed the last drop in the thermos lid. "If we don't get lost. And if we find a stream. And if we don't get hurt or eaten by wild animals. If nothing goes wrong."

He nodded and folded the map back into his pocket. "It's a risk either way."

Even though her stomach was comfortably filled with half a thermos of coffee, Sam experienced an abrupt irrational thirst. It was going to get worse.

"You think we should try to walk out, don't you?"

That's why he'd built the stone arrow and amassed their supplies.

"Are you up to it?"

Her eyes flashed. "Anything you can do, Bannister, I can do!"

His laugh crinkled the purple bruise into tiny pleats. "That's my girl."

"I just don't want to," she finished.

Smiling, he covered her hand with his. "I'm not crazy about being earthbound either. Think of it as a camping trip. Didn't you ever go camping? With the girl scouts or something?"

His hand over hers felt warm and strong and right. "Not with the girl scouts. But my father took me a couple of times." When his eyebrow rose, she shrugged slightly and a crooked smile curved her lips. "I think my father always wanted a son."

"And you tried to be that son?" When she shifted uncomfortably, Luke quietly stroked her hand. "It's early. We don't have to make a decision yet. We'll talk awhile then we'll decide on our next step. Tell me about being Frank Adams' son."

Sam drew a breath and frowned at the sweeping slopes rising sharply from the meadow floor. She couldn't imagine climbing them. Hoping the idea would settle and take hold if she gave it a few minutes, she turned her thoughts backward.

"My parents were older than most parents," she began slowly. Lifting a stick, she drew aimless patterns in the dirt. "Mom and Dad had given up on having any children. I wasn't born until they were both in their middle forties. They thought I was a miracle."

"So do I," Bannister smiled.

"I could do no wrong. They thought whatever I did was wonderful. They still do." She waited for him to make a frivolous comment.

Instead, he looked at her for a long moment then said quietly. "That's a big responsibility—feeling like you can't make a mistake."

She stared at him in surprise. "That's it exactly." A rush of emotion raised an embarrassing moisture to her eyes and she quickly dropped her gaze. Luke Bannister was the last person on earth she would have expected to understand. But he'd grasped immediately what she was saying.

"And I always thought you only children had it easy," he said lightly.

"Nope," she answered, collecting herself. "All my life I've tried to live up to my parent's expectations. I've tried to be all the things they wanted me to be."

"Have you succeeded?"

Her head fell backward, tumbling dark curls down her back. "No. Mom wants me to get married and have children . . ."

"I'm going to like your mother."

". . . so I've disappointed her. And Dad wants me to make a success of Adams Air—and I'm disappointing him."

Luke slid an arm around her shoulders, but she shrugged it off. She didn't want his pity or his sympathy. It was her problem and she would work it out. After a moment, she asked, "What was it like growing up in a large family?"

"Loud," he laughed. "But some of the problems are the same. No one likes to disappoint their parents, darlin'."

Already she regretted opening this topic. A tightness had returned to her chest, a familiar dread of failure stirred in a dark corner of her mind. She shook off the feeling with difficulty.

"My dad hoped I'd be a cattle rancher like my brothers." He gazed at the mountaintops as Sam

looked up curiously. "He can't understand my commitment to flying."

"Surely your parents understand that you have to
live your own life."

"Yes, they do." Luke examined her eyes. "Do you
understand that, darlin'? Are you doing what
Samantha Adams wants to do? Or are you living
someone else's dream?"

Their eyes held. And suddenly Sam experienced
difficulty remembering what they had been discussing. She stared into his warm concern, and intimate images whirled in her mind. She remembered
his solid chest pressed to her spine, his muscled
thighs cradling her body, her cheek nestling into his
large palm.

Abruptly she pushed to her feet and smoothed her
hands across her slacks. "Come on, Bannister, move
it. We've got a long walk ahead of us."

He stood and she felt the tension of his nearness as
he placed his hands on her shoulders. "Thank you for
taking me in last night. Seems to me that I remember . . ."

Frowning, she spun from the pressure of his fingers. "You were freezing, anyone would have rescued you." Summoning a shaky smile, she looked up
at him. "I don't want you getting sick on me. Not
until I learn how to work this compass watch."

Laughing, he led her to the row of items beside the
plane. "Okay, these are backpacks." He lifted the
piles of nylon webbing and shook them out as Sam
nodded soberly.

Minutes later, she lifted her arms as he adjusted
the load against her shoulders then bent to tie the
webbing at her waist.

"Comfortable?"

"You're kidding."

He smiled. "Tolerable, then?"

"I guess it has to be." She'd insisted on carrying her share of the weight. Looking at him, she suppressed a smile. "You look like the hunchback of Notre Dame." The tarp rose above his improvised pack, hanging over his cap; he squinted through his black eye.

They looked around to be certain they hadn't forgotten anything, then quizzed each other to double-check.

"You taped a note inside the plane?"

"Yes. You've got the map? The lighter?"

"The thermos? Your sweater?"

Sam bent to the ground, the weight of the pack nearly toppling her. When she rose, she extended her hand and gave him a pebble. "Suck on it. You won't feel as thirsty."

"Not bad," he said admiringly. "How come I didn't think of that?"

She looked pained, then slid on her sunglasses and watched him do the same. One of his lenses was cracked.

"Ready?" she asked. For a brief instant, she wanted to huddle against the fuselage. However inadequate the site was, it was safe and familiar. The idea of striking out into the unknown wilderness turned her knees to water.

"Let's go."

She watched him stride past her, pushing aside the tall mountain grasses with his boots. Beneath the towering shapes jutting toward the sky he looked as small and insignificant as Sam felt.

Sam chewed her lip and comforted herself by listing a dozen things that would have made their situation worse. One or both of them could have been injured on impact. She could have been wearing a skirt and high heels. They could have crashed in the dead of winter. They might not have had a knife or a lighter or a map.

Realizing she was simply delaying the inevitable, she straightened and adjusted the weight on her shoulders. Breathing deeply of the crisp fall air, she let her gaze travel across a carpet of nodding wildflowers and then toward a rustling stand of pine and bright golden aspen. It was a glorious autumn morning.

"A good day for a hike," she murmured. Then she ducked her head and set out down the mountain.

Chapter Seven

"I've never been so tired in my life!" Sam eased the pack from her shoulders and fell to the ground, leaning her back against a tree trunk. "I ache in places I didn't know I had."

Smiling, Luke dropped beside her and rested against the trunk. "I'll bet we covered eight or nine miles."

"Is that all?" Sam felt as if she'd been walking for days, for weeks. She could scarcely remember a time when she hadn't concentrated on placing one weary step after another.

"They were hard miles."

"Straight up and straight down." Gratefully, she sipped from the thermos lid, then returned it to him. Easing off her shoes, she wiggled her toes and winced. "I think I'm getting a blister."

"I'll look at it in a minute."

Now that she'd rested and slaked her thirst, Sam felt better than she had in hours. "I'll live, Luke. This isn't the place for chivalry."

"Darlin', we need to talk about this."

"About what?"

"About you being so prickly every time I try to help you." He rolled his head along the tree trunk and looked into her eyes. "We're dependent on each other now. I help you and you help me. If we're going to get out of here, we need to draw on each other's strengths."

Sam dropped her eyes and considered. He was

right, of course. Pride insisted that she not be a
burden—she'd resisted his assistance up rocks and
across fallen logs. Perhaps she was being foolish,
taking unnecessary risks.

"You're right," she sighed.

"I'm glad we've settled that. You scared me half to
death coming down that shale slide."

Sam grinned. "I scared *me* half to death."

They talked about the day's obstacles for a few
minutes then Luke pushed to his feet. "If you feel up
to it, I think we should set up camp for the night."

She didn't think she could move, but she nodded
anyway. The sun had dipped below the mountain
ridge, and a chill had settled in the shadows. Soon
the temperature would plunge toward the thirties.

In comfortable silence they applied themselves to
making camp, working in harmony with an economy
of motion and discussion. When the tent was erected
and a cheerful fire crackled in the pit, Sam sliced the
apple into thin wedges and laid them on squares of
tarp beside a small handful of chips. They had eaten
the chocolate raisins for lunch. She was acutely
aware that they had nothing else and were a long
way from their next meal.

Bannister popped an apple slice into his mouth.
"Did you ever notice how married people automatically divide chores? Without even talking about it?"

"We aren't married, Luke."

"Not yet."

She looked at him from across the fire and narrowed her eyes. "Are you going to start that again?"

"I never quit," he grinned.

After tying her scarf over her hair, Sam tilted her
head and studied him. "You know, you really do look
like Clark Gable." His pained expression raised a
smile to her lips.

"Frankly, my dear, I don't give a damn."

"You've heard it before, right?"

"All my life. That's why I don't wear a mustache."

"When did you first . . . ?"

The conversation drifted into stories of growing up. His centered around a large, close-knit family, hers were a hodge-podge of girlish tea parties and tomboyish roughhousing.

Bannister shook his head, smiling as she pulled on her extra sweater and buttoned her jacket. "I can picture you as the homecoming queen, but I can't imagine you sliding into third base."

Sam was oddly pleased. Although she reminded herself that it would be better if her business adversary viewed her as competitive and aggressively tough, she liked it that he saw her feminine qualities.

Lapsing into silence, she tried to sort through her reactions to their discussion. As tall as she was, there were few men who made her feel truly feminine. She knew it was silly, but she tended to equate femininity with small women, the type who wore ruffles and managed to look helpless and cute. Sam scorned ruffles, and she didn't consider herself helpless or cute. She was competent, efficient, and bright. It surprised her a little that Bannister seemed to think these qualities engagingly feminine. It was a new perspective.

Holding her hands out to the fire, she smiled at him then said softly, "Now it's your turn. Tell me about Vietnam. Was it terrible?"

"It was terrible."

After a pause, he began in a low flat voice, staring into the flames. And gradually he became so immersed in memory that Sam wondered if he remembered that she was listening. After a hesitant beginning, the words poured from him in a torrent of pain and anger that gathered momentum as the night slipped away. He spoke of planes hurtling toward earth in spirals of smoke and flame, of men marching away never to return. He talked of mud and jungle and insects and fear, an ever-present fear that seared men's souls. Eyes hard, he stared into the fire and talked quietly of men named Bill and José and Chip and Ace, men he'd known well, men who hadn't come back. His voice cracked on a whisper and he halted abruptly.

At some point in his story, Sam had moved from the far side of the fire to sit beside him. There was no comfort she could offer, no words that wouldn't have sounded trite or superfluous. All she could do was hold his hand and try not to cry out when his fingers tightened in a painful grip.

"How long have I been talking?" he demanded, blinking at her.

"I don't know. It doesn't matter." The moist shine in his eyes reached out to her heart, and she thought of all he had seen, all he had endured. No wonder the wide freedom of the limitless sky called to him.

"Sam . . ." He pushed a hand through the black curls framing his face. "Forgive me for . . . I've never talked about it before. I've never been able to talk about . . ."

"Shhh. It's all right." She opened her arms to him, and held him close to her body, feeling the tremor rippling along his flesh. The action was natural, automatic, performed without further thought than that he needed her.

His arms tightened, catching the end of her scarf and pulling it from her head. He buried his face in her tousled hair and pressed her close to his heart, as if she anchored his reality and pulled him back from the dark caverns of memory.

Sam offered herself without reservation, sensing the passage of strength from herself to him. Soothing sounds issued from the back of her throat; she stroked his hair quietly, feeling a tremble begin in her own fingers. Never in her life had she experienced such a deep sensation of sharing, of looking so deeply into another human being.

When his lips found hers, she didn't resist, but lifted her mouth to his warmth, wanting the bond between them to remain unbroken. Her hands framed his face, feeling the scratchiness of his unshaven cheeks, the straight, firm line of his jaw. And through her jacket and extra sweater, she felt his large square hands pressing her against his chest even as she reacted to the urgency building in their kiss.

They were alone in the middle of nowhere. Caught in a vast, raw wilderness with only their small fire and each other to offer against the cold and darkness.

"Sam. My beautiful Sam," he murmured against her parted lips. He smoothed the hair back from her cheek and looked at the firelight glowing over her sunburned skin.

"Oh, Luke." His kisses spread a weakness through her stomach and then a flaming urgency as his mouth grew more insistent and a fiery tingle shot through her body. "Luke . . ."

His name died on her lips as his mouth, his full, warm mouth covered hers and his powerful arms tightened around her. His hands cradled her head as the need in his kisses intensified and flamed into a wild, raw passion matched only by her own mounting need.

Without being aware of moving, they stood, and Sam pressed along his hard muscled length, adjusting herself into the frame of his body, feeling his desire strong against her thighs. A soft groan emerged from his lips as his hands slipped beneath

her jacket and rose to cup her trembling breasts. She
bit back a low cry as her nipples grew as taut as
small pebbles and thrust hard against his palms.

"Sam . . ." he murmured, his lips brushing her eyelids, her cheeks, the corners of her lips.

"Yes," she whispered hoarsely. "Yes, yes, yes." She
opened her eyes and stared at the vast canopy of bril-
liant stars twinkling through the overhanging pines.
"Oh, yes."

Almost dazed, she followed him into the tent and
stretched out across the pine boughs he'd gathered
for their bed. She sensed his solid strength beside
her, felt him gazing down into her face. Then she
opened her arms and drew his mouth to hers, darting
her tongue past his lips to explore within. His kisses
tasted faintly of sweet apple juice, tasted of urgency
and fire and growing passion.

And then, when their frantic kisses could no
longer satisfy their needs, when hands sought and
stroked and trembled and urged, then they kicked
out of jeans and slacks and he reached to slide the
wisp of lace from her hips.

"Sam." His voice was hoarse in her ear, his breathing as ragged and uneven as her own. "Are you
sure?"

She'd never been as sure. And she didn't want to
question, not now. Not when her nerves tingled at
the sensation of his large, rough hands on her body,
when her blood rushed through her veins like a river
of fire. Not when she felt the near pain of an emptiness demanding to be filled. Her arms circled his
neck, drawing him down to her in a kiss that left her
shaken by its intensity, by its deep expression of
need.

His fingers traveled lightly over her bared stomach, raising a shiver of longing in their path. And he
teased her into trembling readiness by circling his

fingertips ever nearer the dark triangle, skillfully trailing up the inside of her pale thighs, then retreating until a sound midway between a scream and a sob groaned from her throat.

"Please, please," she whispered. "Luke . . ." Her own fingers lifted to the dark line of hair pointing down his stomach, and she followed it until her hand found his velvety strength. Her fingers closed around a warm rigidity as he groaned and she guided him into her.

A sound tore from her as he entered, filling the vast emptiness with heat and strength and urgency. And it was right, it was as perfectly right as she'd known it would be in a small, sheltered corner of her mind. Their bodies fit as if fashioned for each other, and he seemed to sense her needs as she sensed his. Dimly, she was aware that he paced himself to her rhythms, that he held back until a soft sheen of perspiration appeared on her brow and her body arched up to meet his thrust with a wildness that signaled and spoke to him.

Understanding, he increased the pace, bringing her to the edge of something wild and hot and wonderful. And he held her there, on the rim of a sweetness she comprehended only dimly as he let himself go, let himself approach that edge also. And then, they burst forth together and the world seemed to shatter and reassemble behind Sam's eyes, expanding and contracting in waves of ecstasy that swept her flaming body in shudders so intensely sweet they were almost painful.

As if from a great distance, she felt his head drop to her shoulder, heard his raw breath against her hair. And she wished they could stay like this forever, hearts pounding furiously as one, their spent breath mingled, their arms holding one another against the night.

When she could breathe normally, Sam hastily drew on her slacks, suddenly shy. And she turned her back to him as she adjusted her sweater and rebuttoned her jacket. She heard the rustle of his jeans as he pulled them on.

"Sam?"

"Ummm."

"I love you."

Tears sprang to her eyes and she had no idea why. Choking, she lowered her head. "Don't say that. It just complicates everything."

Gently, he drew her into his arms then laid back on the soft boughs, pillowing her head on his shoulder. The scent of crushed pine rose around them as he stroked her cheek with his thumb.

Sam's mind raced backward, trying to discover another moment when she'd shared such a deep intimacy with another person. She recalled nothing remotely similar.

"Someone hurt you. Who was it?"

"Brad Jennings," she blurted, before she had a chance to make her usual concealing excuses. Brad's image called forth a familiar rush of pain. The hurt didn't center on losing him as much as on his betrayal of her trust. She couldn't believe she was confessing this. She'd never told anyone what had ended her brief engagement, not even her parents. "He said he loved me, but . . . all he really wanted was Adams Air. Not me."

For a time Brad Jennings had been the center of her world. She'd given him her trust, her future, and her love. In return Brad had offered lukewarm promises and an eagerness to climb the ladder in one leap. His ambitions were firmly fixed on Adams Air. The day Sam broke their engagement, she'd sworn never again to let a man into her life except on a casual basis. She didn't want quick promises and she didn't need pretty words that meant nothing. Most of all, she didn't want to be hurt again.

Until now, she hadn't been tempted to break her vow.

"Jennings was a fool," Luke said flatly. He turned her face up to his and kissed her softly, tenderly. "I love you, Samantha Adams."

"Don't say that."

"I love the looks of you, the sound of you. I love the way you adapt."

She pushed the past back where it belonged and smiled against his chest. "I bitched every step of the way. How can you say that?"

"The point is, darlin', you took the risk. And you held up your end. You're bright and beautiful and stubborn and sharp-tongued and . . ."

Her smile widened into a grin. "Stubborn and sharp-tongued? Is that why you want to marry me?" The words startled her. They lent credibility to his nonsense, and that wasn't what she wanted. Was it?

"That's part of it. I don't want a woman who'll let herself be steamrolled by anyone. Not even me."

Sam pressed her fingertips flat on his chest, feeling the steady, strong beat of his heart against her palm. Her body felt languid and warm, sated and limp. And she felt as if she'd known Luke Bannister longer than anyone else among her friends and acquaintances, better than she had ever known Brad. The thought surprised her and raised a dozen disturbing questions. After a wide yawn, she snuggled into his warmth and her lashes sank. She'd think about all this in the daylight, when issues didn't seem so clouded.

"Sleepy?" he whispered against her temple.

"Mmmm."

Shifting onto his side, Luke wrapped his large frame around her curled body, sheltering her from the cold draft seeping beneath the tent edge. One arm pillowed her head, the other lay across her body.

"Sam?"

"Hmmm?"

"Do you have breasts in there?"

She felt his grin against her hair and smiled in return. "Breasts you wouldn't believe, buster." In proof she raised his hand and cupped it over her jacket front.

"I believe it," he sighed happily. "Now go to sleep. You're keeping me awake with all this chatter."

Laughing softly, she pressed into his cradle of warmth and covered his hand on her breast with slim fingers. And she slept better than she had in years.

Chapter Eight

Luke woke her with a light kiss behind her ear and Sam blinked, then smiled up at him.

"Darlin', if you keep looking at me like that, I'm going to forget everything but you and burn our breakfast."

"What breakfast? I thought we ate everything last night." Yawning hugely, Sam rubbed her eyes then crawled out of the tent and stretched. Despite a dozen small scrapes and bruises, her body didn't protest as it had before and she decided that roughing it was toning up her deskbound muscles. Her smile of optimism vanished at Luke's reply.

"Roasted grasshoppers." He bent beside the coals and used a stick to push at a pile of small brown things crisping in the metal platter.

"Good God! Grasshoppers?" Sam's full lips twisted in revulsion; she squeezed her eyes shut.

"Chock full of protein," Luke answered cheerfully. "And easy to catch. Grasshoppers go dormant at night. They don't wake until the sun warms them so they're easy pickings if you get to them before the sun does."

Sam leaned to stare at the roasting insects then shuddered violently. Her stomach looped in a queasy roll. "No way, Bannister. I'm not going to eat bugs."

"Suit yourself, darlin'." He nodded toward a square of tarp. "We also have a few wild strawberries for my lady's pleasure."

Sam inspected the pitifully few berries. The last of

the season's crop, they were small and wizened, about as appetizing as lumps of pink stone. She was hungry enough to consider eating them. Dropping to a log, Sam propped her chin in her hands and risked a peek at the grasshoppers.

"How do you know when they're done?"

"They're done now. Want some?" He shared out the roast grasshoppers and the berries, placing them on the tarp squares.

When he casually popped a handful into his mouth, Sam could hear them crunching in the morning stillness.

"That's disgusting!" But if Bannister could eat grasshoppers, then so could she. Damn. Shuddering, Sam lifted a shapeless brown crisp between her fingers. She decided it was better not to look at it. "I can't believe I'm doing this." Closing her eyes, she pushed the repulsive thing between her lips and bit down. Then she hastily chewed one of the sour little strawberries. "Ugh!"

"You're right. We could use some salt."

"*Salt?* We could use some bacon and eggs and hash browns and coffee." She stared as Luke calmly ate his share of the grasshoppers and berries. "I'll say this for you, Bannister, you've got to be the easiest man in the world to cook for. If you'll eat bugs, you'll eat anything." She smiled.

Clark Gable's lopsided grin widened his lips. "That's right. I told you there were a lot of things about me that you were going to love. I pick up my socks too."

She finished her share of the grasshoppers and berries and decided after the initial shock of knowing what she was eating that grasshoppers weren't all that bad. Not good, but bearable.

"You're being a good sport about this, darlin'," Luke said when she made a show of blotting her lips and pretending she'd just enjoyed a gourmet breakfast.

Sam shrugged. "What else can we do? There's no point in complaining." She'd never grasped the logic in protesting the unchangeable. Like Luke, she was a person who coped. The thought startled her and she stared at him a moment, privately admitting that she was glad Luke Bannister faced her across the coals instead of most of the people she knew. She could think of few who would have faced the obstacles with the confidence and optimism Luke had consistently displayed. Or his unfailing good humor.

Luke squinted at the sun, then stood and scooped dirt over the coals. "Time to hit the trail, partner."

"Okay. But today I pack the backpacks. Deal?" Without waiting for his amused consent, Sam laid their supplies in a row and considered thoughtfully, occasionally testing an item for bulk and weight. She experienced a glow of satisfaction when Luke turned to her with surprise after strapping his pack in place.

"Did you forget something?" When Sam smiled and shook her head, he raised a suspicious eyebrow. "You threw something out?"

"Nope. I just organized us—distributed the load more evenly."

His sunburned gaze filled with admiration. "I can't wait to see what you'll do with my office." He turned downhill and his next words floated up to her in the bright morning air. "The sooner the better."

Sam frowned at the mention of his office. Thus far, they had tactfully refrained from discussing business. Their campfire talk had centered on personal subjects, exploring past experiences, news issues, mutual likes and dislikes. And Sam preferred to keep it that way, she concluded, as she pushed aside a pine branch and sidestepped down a steep incline.

Alone in the wilderness, they had to trust each other, had to depend on each other. Keying on their differences could only disrupt the harmony they needed to survive.

Concentrating on her footing, Sam followed Luke's lead as the sun climbed in the sky. She skirted fallen aspens, climbed granite boulders, waded through slanting meadows of tall grass and wildflowers. When she stopped to wipe her forehead, she heard Luke's cheerful whistling as he consulted the map and their makeshift compass.

He blew her a kiss then adjusted his cap and pushed through a growth of low brush. Without warning the same deep sense of intimacy and warmth they had shared last night swept Sam's emotions. She knew this man, knew who and what he was, his strengths and his weaknesses. And he knew her. They were sharing an intense experience that had created a strong bond of trust and friendship and . . . love?

Catching her lip between her teeth, Sam drew a long breath. Luke had said that he loved her. But did he? Or was he simply reacting to the drama of an unusual situation? And what of her own feelings?

For an instant the crimson emblem of Adams Air flashed before Sam's eyes, swiftly followed by the Bannister Air eagle. Resolutely, she squashed the images, then adjusted her pack, ducked her head, and strode on.

But her thoughts warily circled the subject she couldn't push from her mind. Annoyed with herself, Sam paused at the rim of a boulder field and watched Luke climb a rock as large as a house.

"I love you," she whispered haltingly, testing the words on her tongue from the safety of distance. She smiled at her gullibility. Clark Gable notches up another conquest. Still, she could no longer protest that they didn't know each other. Disaster underscored the best and the worst in people; they were seeing each other exposed.

Tilting her head, Sam shaded her eyes and grinned at Bannister. He stood, legs straddled, atop the giant boulder. Cupping his hands around his mouth, he released an echoing Tarzan yell, fists beating his chest, then he threw back his head and laughed as a cloud of birds rose from the trees and flapped toward quieter roosts.

"Not bad," Sam commented when she had pulled herself up beside him. "But listen to this." Her own Tarzan yell soared and spread over the green and gold valley below them.

"How about a duet?"

Together they yelled, choking on laughter, and agreed that few things had ever felt as good as standing on a chunk of granite and shouting to the world. Competing, they vied to outdo one another with Tarzan yells, then they attempted yodeling, their efforts hilarious failures.

"Please stop, I can't stand any more." Sam held her aching side and wiped tears of laughter from her eyes. "Besides scaring away the wildlife for miles around, we're only making ourselves more thirsty."

Sitting, they leaned back to back, using each other for support as Luke poked at the map and aligned Sam's watch with the noonday sun. He stood so abruptly that Sam nearly fell over.

"Sam, darlin'," he said excitedly. Shading his eyes, he stared hard down the mountainside. "Unless I flunk trailblazing, there should be a stream down there."

All she could see was the tops of the trees, a soft blanket of rippling green and orange, and occasionally a flaming column of autumn scarlet. But when she brushed back her hair she could hear the faint gurgling spill of tumbling water.

Her eyes lit and she smiled delightedly up into Luke's bearded face. "First one there gets a bath." Her mouth felt as parched as her sunburned cheeks. The thirst she'd been denying suddenly seemed overwhelming.

"We'll make camp early."

"Agreed."

"We'll drink until we slosh, then I'll catch you the biggest trout you ever saw." Luke jumped from the rock and held up his arms to her.

His hands circled her waist and he slid her slowly down the front of his body, holding her tightly against his chest and hips. His vibrant blue eyes caressed her parted lips, the hollow pulsing at the base of her throat.

"Luke . . ." Her fingers tightened on the muscles swelling beneath her hands as his wide mouth covered hers. Then he touched her sunburned nose and smiled, and she tugged his beard and laughed softly with the happiness of being in his arms, of feeling the crisp autumn sunshine in her hair, of knowing they were only minutes from water.

Eagerly they crashed down the mountainside, shouting and calling to each other. And when they reached the stream, they threw off their packs and dropped to their knees on the bank, scooping handfuls of clear, icy water into their mouths, laughing and splashing like children.

Luke was first to strip off his shirt and jeans and wade naked into the rush of water tumbling over the rocks upstream. Sam's breath caught as she stared at his bronzed chest and the pale white beneath. An involuntary stirring heated her stomach.

"Come on in, darlin', the water's fine."

"Like hell. Your lips are turning blue."

He grinned. "Then come here and warm me up."

Sam wouldn't have believed that she'd ever go skinny-dipping with a man. But she did so now. After tugging her sweater over her head, she stepped out of her soiled slacks and stood before Luke's admiring stare in her lacy bra and panties. After a brief hesitation, she unhooked her bra and slid her panties down over her hips.

"My God," Luke whispered hoarsely. "You're the most beautiful woman I've ever seen."

Sam had expected a rush of embarrassment, but it didn't happen. Somehow their nakedness seemed natural and right, as free and open as nature itself. Dropping her arms to her sides, Sam stood before him with shy pride, feeling the dappled sunlight glowing on her hair and skin.

"Come here," Luke said gruffly, opening his arms.

Gingerly, Sam stepped from the bank, intending to walk into his arms. But she froze as the shock of icy water bubbled around her knees, turning her legs a bright pink beneath the water. "Good Lord," she gasped. "It's freezing!" Goosebumps erupted over her skin.

"You'll get used to it in a minute."

Her dark eyes widened as she watched him bend to scoop up a handful of water and she edged backward. "Don't you dare, Luke Bannister." He grinned at her. "I mean it!"

She ducked and shrieked as cold water cascaded over her shoulders and trickled between her breasts.

"Okay, Bannister, this is war." Bending, she hurled handfuls of icy water at his chest and thighs, dodging when he splashed her in return.

When they were both soaked and panting with laughter and exertion, they hastily washed each other, then scrambled up the bank and flung their shivering bodies atop the long soft grass where the sun could reach them.

And then, when the golden sun had kissed them dry and warm, they made slow glorious love beside the stream, tender with each other and unhurried. Reveling in the sensual touch of naked skin against naked skin, of making love in the open air, they eagerly explored each other's bodies, murmuring soft cries of delight as they discovered small secrets, as they learned where and how to give and receive the greatest pleasure.

Sam discovered she could arouse him by nibbling his stomach; Luke found the sensitive area below her left breast. Closing her dark lashes, Sam trailed her fingers along the twin ropes of muscle defining his spine. And she shivered rapturously as his lips nuzzled between her breasts then trailed across her stomach, lazily teasing.

A blissful smile parted her lips, and her fingers wound into his black hair as she moaned softly and arched against the tantalizing brush of his lips. A slow fire ignited in her flesh and spread a sheen of liquid flame along her skin as warm and compelling as the autumn sunshine drifting through the aspens overhead.

A whisper of rustling leaves and the seductive murmur of the stream filled her ears, along with the quickened rush of their breath. Then his tongue found her center and she gasped and her slender hips lifted to him as if they possessed a will of their own.

"Luke," she murmured. "Oh, Luke . . ."

He teased her and loved her until her body quivered like an arrow taut against the master's bow. And when she cried out for him, when she felt as if she would explode with joy and passion, he rose above her and she wrapped her long legs around his hips and guided him into her, meeting his thrusts with a glad cry. They drank deep kisses from each other's lips and Sam opened herself to him with a completeness she'd never before experienced.

And then the world spun wide in an eruption of golden-edged darkness before collapsing in on itself to leave her breathless and shaken and wondrous. Above her, Luke tensed and thrust forward, her name on his lips, then he too lay spent and gasping for breath.

After a moment he pushed up on his elbows and smiled down at her, his eyes as soft as blue velvet. "I love you," he said simply.

"I—I love you too."

"I knew you would. I'm the best deal you're ever going to find, an ugly girl like you."

She laughed up at him, her dark eyes shining, thinking his beard made him look like a pirate or a mountain man.

"Sam?"

"Hmmm?" Lazily she decided she could remain like this forever, safe in his arms with the sun warm on her skin, his weight on her hips. The scent of pine spiced each breath; the stream gurgled happily. And it was impossible to believe their survival had ever been in doubt. This was not an ordeal, but an idyllic interlude, a lovely fantasy.

"There's something I forgot to tell you about eating grasshoppers." He brushed a strand of hair from her cheek and smiled, gazing into her eyes.

"Ugh." Sam wrinkled her nose. "What did you forget?"

"Grasshopper breath." His smile widened into a grin. "You've got it."

She smacked him on the shoulder with her fist, then rolled to her feet and gave him a mock glare. "So do you. What we haven't got is a trout for dinner." The promise of food reminded her that she was ravenous. "You get us a trout and I'll find some wild mint to counteract the effects of breakfast."

"It's a deal." But he made no effort to rise. Instead Luke stretched in the sun, folded his hands behind his dark head, and watched her dress, an expression of lazy contentment on his face. "Sam, I want you to know this has been one of the happiest days of my life."

She popped her head through the neck of her sweater and smiled at him, her eyes soft and glowing. "Me too." It was true. She'd shed the inhibitions and limitations of civilized existence without thinking about it. She'd enjoyed a day of glorious freedom from artificial restraints. And it had been wonderful. Bending, she brushed his lips gently, then jumped back and smiled when he reached for her.

"Dinner, remember? The biggest trout I ever saw?"

"Slave driver."

While she unpacked their supplies and prepared to dig a fire pit, Luke patiently sharpened a long aspen branch to a tapering point. Standing, he raised the branch to his shoulder, testing the balance and weight.

"You're going to spear a fish?" Sam asked incredulously.

"Nothing to it."

"This I've got to see." She followed him downstream to a point where the water collected in a deep calm pool, then she sat on a flat rock while he rolled up his jeans and waded into the stream.

Luke waited patiently, his eyes scanning the water, the branch poised at his shoulder. Then he gave a shout and hurled the spear.

The spear stuck in the stream bottom, the shaft quivering above the rushing water. Sam smiled at the sky as he released a string of curses before retrieving the spear to begin again.

On the second throw the spear slid along the stream bottom then caught in the current and bobbed away.

Bannister watched it go, hands on hips, a scowl drawing his brow. "There's a flaw here."

"You work it out, Tarzan. I'll get the fire going."

"Hmmm," he responded absently, pulling at the stubble on his chin.

When Luke returned two hours later, he called her name and proudly exhibited a glistening rainbow trout. Then he saw what she was doing and his jaw dropped.

Sam looked up from the fire and smiled. "Very nice," she said sweetly. Then she poked a stick at the four plate-sized trout she was roasting on the metal platter.

"How did you do that?" Bannister demanded. He stalked to the fire and stared down at the fish.

"I made a trap."

"Show me."

Sam led him upstream and pointed to the conical trap she'd fashioned from limber aspen twigs and tape. Two fat trout swam within the enclosure. "There's breakfast."

"Did your dad teach you how to do that?"

"Nope. Girl scouts."

He nodded. "You know," he said slowly, "my father is right. He's always claimed that the smartest thing about the Bannister men is the women they marry."

Sam inclined her head. "I'm impressed by your graciousness in the face of defeat."

"Defeat, hell. I got one, didn't I?"

She glanced at his frown and her smile wavered. The competitiveness between them flashed very near the surface. "Yes, you did," she conceded softly. She didn't want anything to mar this perfect day. "And you did it the hard way. I wish I'd been there to see it."

"Don't patronize me, Sam."

"I'm not. To be honest, I didn't think you could do it."

He sighed and to Sam's relief his smile reappeared. "I didn't. I gave up on the damned spear. I caught the trout—scooped it up and threw it out on the bank."

"Luke, why are we standing here talking? I'm so hungry I could eat the bark off that tree."

He inhaled deeply. "I never smelled anything as wonderful as your fish. Let's go."

They ate until they were stuffed and toasted each other with gulps of icy, sparkling water. When they finished, every scrap of the flaky white meat had vanished. All that remained was a pile of delicate bones which Luke buried on the stream bank.

When he returned, Sam provided spiny leaves of wild mint to chew. "Lest we exchange grasshopper breath for trout breath," she explained.

After slipping into their jackets, they stretched out on the grass beside the fire pit and watched the sun's orange globe sink below the mountaintops.

"That was the best meal I've ever eaten, darlin'. My compliments to the chef."

"Wait until you discover what I can do with a lamb chop."

"Ah, but you haven't experienced heaven until you've tasted one of my Bannister specials. Steak this thick smothered with mushrooms and onions."

"Or the Italian food at Little Pepinas in North Denver. Now that's heaven. Have you been there?"

After arguing the merits of favorite restaurants, they drifted into other topics, ranging easily from music to travel to whatever popped into their minds, discovering a pleasing similarity of tastes and inclinations.

When the fire had burned low and the mountains were an ebony shadow against the star-bright canopy of the sky, Luke asked softly. "Do you believe in God, Sam?"

She nestled her head against the pillow of matted grass and stared upward at the winking stars. "Yes." She'd never been able to believe that something as wonderful as a puppy had occurred by accident. Or a snowflake. Or the fullness of a human heart.

"I do too. Moments like this reaffirm my faith."

Sam smiled into a comfortable silence. "But do you believe in Willie Nelson, now that's the important question."

His chuckle drifted from above the glowing bed of coals. "Absolutely. In my heart I know that Willie is alive and well somewhere in Texas or Nashville."

Rolling onto her side, Sam cast him a slow seductive glance from beneath her long lashes. "How about you, Luke Bannister? Are you alive and well?"

His eyes smoldered into hers and his voice dropped to a rich husky register. "Shall I prove it?"

Smiling, Sam opened her arms.

Chapter Nine

❧

Neither was eager to break camp the following morning. They lingered over a breakfast of roast trout and hot mint tea, waiting for the sun to burn off the silvery coat of frost sparkling on the foliage.

"It feels like an early winter," Sam commented. The night had been the coldest yet. She'd awakened to cheeks and fingers pink with cold.

"I'm glad we have the fire." Luke brewed more mint tea and refilled the thermos lid.

Sam accepted it gratefully, sipping the warmth slowly before sharing the cup. Colorado's weather was capable of swinging from high afternoon temperatures to cold nights, and nowhere was this more so than in the mountains. An electric blanket would have felt good last night.

Smiling at the thought, she idly touched the sunburn peeling across her forehead and nose and cheeks, welcoming the return of the sun. Edging closer to the fire, she watched as early morning light struck silver along Luke's temples and caught in the gray streaking his beard. A thick dark stubble hid his chin and lower cheeks, soft to the touch now instead of scratchy.

"Do you think the Civil Air Patrol is looking for us by now?" she asked.

"I imagine so." Unhurried, Luke assembled their supplies near the packs. "I think we'll stumble across Leadville sometime tomorrow in any case."

"Tomorrow," Sam repeated softly. A strange conflicting tumble of emotions rose in her thoughts. On the one hand, she longed for a hot, sudsy tub, a shampoo, and a change of clothing. Plus a good night's sleep on a soft mattress. And her toothbrush. She could picture a pot of coffee so vividly she could almost smell the brew.

On the other hand, she didn't want this idyll to end. Once she'd understood they were in no immediate danger of getting lost or of starving, she'd relaxed almost as if their wandering down the mountain canyons and valleys were a planned outing instead of the consequence of catastrope. Never had she felt as free and uninhibited, or as happy.

A week ago such a thought would not have made sense but now she looked at Luke and knew that it did. She had tested herself against adversity and was pleased with the results. She had proven herself as a person and as a woman. She had shared the innermost thoughts of another person and opened herself as well. And she suspected it couldn't have happened any other way but here and with this man.

Extending her hands, she examined her cracked and broken fingernails then dropped her gaze to her slacks, inspecting the small rips and earth-stained knees. She thought of her peeling face and the multitude of small bruises covering her body. There was no observable reason why she should feel so happy. But she did.

"Remember the field of little purple flowers we found the first day?" She smiled, remembering the bouquet Luke had picked for her.

He nodded, watching her curiously.

"And the deer. Remember the fawn we saw?"

He laughed. "At first you thought it was a bear."

"A small bear." Still smiling, she knelt before the packs and began to divide the load, freshly surprised by how few items were required for survival. A penknife, a lighter, a digging tool . . . and someone to talk to and share the nights with. She found herself wishing life could always be this simple and uncomplicated.

"Luke? Are you getting tired of me?" The words slipped past her lips before she had time to think about them, expressing a fear she hadn't realized she felt.

"Of course not! Whatever made you ask such a thing?"

Sam shrugged. "I don't know. I've never spent this much time with anyone before. I was just wondering if . . ."

Bannister's large hands framed her shoulders as he knelt beside her and turned her to face him.

"Sam, I don't think I could ever get tired of you. Don't you understand even yet? I want to spend my life with you."

"Maybe you won't feel the same when we get home." She searched his gaze, seeking answers to vague, unformed questions.

Luke's black brows rose in puzzled arcs. "Why on earth not? I love you. And Sam"—he tilted her chin with his finger and gazed steadily into her wide eyes—"that isn't going to change."

She stared at him for a moment then threw her arms around his neck and clung to him, not understanding the sharp blade of anxiety piercing her heart. Suddenly she, who had always been competent and insulated, felt vulnerable, helplessly open and unprotected. Nature in its raw state didn't allow for the masks civilization encouraged. Here they were both reduced to the basic elements of personality, unshielded by layers of ambition, sophistication, and all the other artificial qualities people hid behind. They had to rely on each other and trust each other. But she knew it wouldn't be this way always—soon they would take up their masks again.

Her shaking hands rose to press his strong face and she gazed deeply into his eyes. "I wish it could be like this always," she whispered. "I wish all we had to think about was a sheltered campsite and food for supper. And each other." She wished their lives could remain this rockbottom basic without the complications of schedules and balance sheets and which clients belonged to whom.

"Sam . . ." He kissed her then, a gentle lingering kiss that provided the reassurance words could not. His mouth was tender, and he held her as if she were a fragile treasure an abrupt movement could shatter.

Sam buried her face in the warm crease at his neck and closed her eyes, holding him so fiercely that she could feel his steady heartbeat against her breast. Inhaling deeply, she smelled the stream-fresh scent of his skin, drank in the heady fragrance of pine boughs and sunshine. And she vowed to remember this moment always.

"Luke?" she said against his neck. "Will it be the same?"

He understood. "Yes, darlin'. The real world won't come between us, I promise you."

But it did. As she followed him along the stream bank, her pack riding smoothly on her shoulders, the real world invaded Sam's thoughts. She climbed when she had to climb, slid when she had to slide, strode forward when the ground momentarily leveled. And she did so automatically, with a minimum of conscious thought. Her mind jumped forward.

Her desk would be mounded with paperwork when she returned: calls, memos, bills of lading, letters to answer, invoices to pay. Marva, her secretary, would be harried and frantic. Her parents would be worried to death. And there was still the loss of Chilton's account to assess. On the personal side, she thought of the townhouse association meeting she had missed and wondered how great an assessment they had voted for the new roof. She hoped her goldfish were still alive.

Every step carrying her nearer to civilization also brought her closer to the problems she'd temporarily set aside. Her dwindling book of business, her ambitions, her desire to make her father proud . . .

By the time they agreed to camp for the night, a tight line had appeared between Sam's dark eyebrows and depression hovered at the edge of her thoughts. When she glanced into Luke's troubled blue gaze, she read a reflection of her own emerging concerns. He too had jumped ahead in his mind.

Wearily they slid the packs from their shoulders and sank to a grassy incline. As if by mutual consent, they delayed pitching the tent and establishing the campsite. Instead, they sat in silence, watching the stream swirl over rocks, break into bubbles, then dance on down the mountain.

When the silence made Sam uneasy, she pushed a hand through her tangled hair then rested her cheek on her upraised knee and looked at him. "Will losing the Fairchild affect your schedules?"

Luke continued to watch the water, his face expressionless. "I may have to give you back Chilton's account."

"I'll service Chilton until you can settle the insurance and arrange for another plane."

"That's generous of you, darlin', and I thank you. But it may not be that simple."

"Why not?" She closed her eyes against her knee and wished they weren't talking about this. She wasn't ready for the real world, even though she knew the discussion was inevitable.

Standing, Luke wandered to the edge of the stream and thrust his hands deeply into his pockets, staring down at the water.

"I don't know if there'll be any insurance money. I'm not certain that High Hopes was insured."

"What?" Sam's head snapped up and she stared in disbelief. "It must be. The bank wouldn't have granted a mortgage without insurance to protect their investment."

"There is no mortgage, Sam. The previous owner offered a cash discount. I planned to finance the plane after it was overhauled."

Sam's head spun. Even considering the plane's age and condition, the cost must have exceeded a hundred thousand dollars. Had Luke leveraged the same money, he could have purchased three planes.

She forced her mind to the insurance issue. "Luke, surely you couldn't have overlooked something as important as insurance. It just isn't possible." Incredulity sharpened her tone.

"I remember the premium notice. I can visualize it on my desk. But I can't recall if I paid it or not."

Sam's hands waved in aimless patterns. "It would have been a large amount of money," she said, hoping to prod his memory. When he shrugged, she tried another angle. "Maybe your secretary paid it?"

"I don't have a secretary."

Bannister was the pilot, salesman, accountant, secretary, and probably the janitor too. Sam shoved a wave of hair behind her ear and bit off the comment she'd been about to make before she examined his slumped shoulders. Still, she could hardly believe what she was hearing. Under no circumstances could she understand how it was possible to overlook a detail as crucial as insurance.

"If you didn't pay the premium, you'll be ruined," she observed quietly.

Luke's shoulders abruptly squared and he tilted his head to look toward the sunset spreading across the western sky. "No, I won't."

"Oh? You can afford to lose all that money?"

"Of course not." He turned then, his eyes hard and determined. "But if I do, Sam, it won't be the end. Only a setback." An ironic grin wavered on his lips. "Admittedly a big setback, but not the end."

"A very big setback."

"And I'll survive it. We won't combine our companies until this matter is cleaned up. I promise you."

A startled expression pinched Sam's face. Her eyes narrowed in appraisal. His words reminded her unpleasantly of Brad Jennings. Whenever Brad had discussed business, an eagerness had glittered in his gaze, his voice had assumed an excitement that hinted he couldn't wait to take the reins of control at Adams Air. The same violently protective urge she'd felt then rose in her chest now.

"We'll see," she said, her voice carefully void of any commitment. "It isn't something we have to decide tonight." Facing away from him, she knelt before the packs and began laying out their digging tool, the thermos, the tape she needed to build a new fish trap. "Are you hungry?" she asked lightly, changing the subject.

"No."

"Me neither." Her appetite had vanished, replaced by a sour taste in the back of her throat. Suddenly she felt bone-weary, too fatigued to face the labor required to build a trap and set up camp.

Fortunately, she didn't have to. Luke set about the tasks with a vengeance, refusing her half-hearted offers of assistance. Almost as if punishing himself, he worked without pause, gouging out a fire pit, then

hammering in the supports for the tent. Sweat trickled down his temples, rivered along his spine.

As watching him made her feel guilty, Sam took
the thermos to the stream and filled it then rocked
back on her heels and stared at the rushing water.

She tried to convince herself that Luke's error was
one anyone could commit. But she didn't believe it.
Competent businessmen didn't make careless mis-
takes, not if they hoped to remain in business. Hers
was a mind trained to detail. In fact, she experienced
great satisfaction knowing she'd earned a reputation
as someone who overlooked nothing. Although she
desperately wanted to understand Luke's business
practices and forgive them, she could find no base
within herself from which to do so. There was no possible circumstances under which she could have
overlooked paying an insurance premium. None.

Troubled, she leaned forward and splashed icy
water over her face, gasping at the cold shock
against her sunburn. The real world had thrust
between herself and Luke by reminding her how different they were. Their values were the same,
and their general outlook—but their differences
assumed an importance in the real world that was
lacking here in the wild. She was a detail person;
Luke was not. She preferred an orderly existence;
order played a small role in Luke's life. Luke was
spontaneous; she was predictable.

Sam's shoulders dropped. Abruptly she was vividly aware of the exhaustion she'd been ignoring.
Her peeling sunburn was raw and painful to the
touch. Her body ached. A happiness she suddenly
distrusted had kept her discomfort at bay, but now it
rushed over her with dismaying intensity. She felt
desperately tired, too weary to move. Her stomach
demanded a balanced meal. And she felt like covering her face with her hands and surrendering to a

storm of confused weeping. Nothing seemed simple and straightforward anymore; doubt flooded her thoughts.

Was Luke another Brad Jennings? A man more interested in Adams Air than in Samantha Adams? She couldn't avoid the fact that a marriage would merge the two companies into a force to be reckoned with. A merger would more than double the size of Bannister Air Freight—and rescue Luke from his insurance difficulties.

Eyes burning, Sam stared at the streambed as she questioned Luke's motives. Had this always been his plan? From the beginning? Did a merger explain why he'd been so attracted to her?

Squeezing her eyes shut, Sam gently rubbed her temples, trying to soothe the start of a headache. A hundred questions sprang into her mind. But no answers.

When Luke sank to the ground beside her, they watched the water without speaking until the golden shadows faded to darkness and a frosty chill in the air drove them to seek the warmth of the fire.

"Do you want to talk?" he asked quietly when the silence between them had lengthened into a painful span.

"Not now, Luke." Sam bit her lip, glancing at him then quickly away. "We're both hungry and exhausted, probably weaker than we realize ..." Her voice trailed into another silence.

Luke drew an audible breath. "You're probably right, Sam," he agreed slowly. "But there's something I have to say and it might as well be now."

She passed him the cup of water, waiting for him to continue.

"I could excuse the insurance fiasco by blaming it on the lack of a secretary or by telling you I was over-worked and too busy to take care of it."

Sam stared into the flames without speaking.

"But that would only be half the truth. The whole truth is that I might very well have overlooked it even under the best of conditions. I hate detail work, Sam, I've never been good at it." His smile didn't reach his eyes. "My father once said it was probably best that I didn't go into ranching—I'd end by misplacing most of the cows."

She glanced at him then and spread her hands in a helpless gesture. "I'm trying to understand, Luke, but I can't. Details don't seem to bother you when you're checking out an airplane—why are they so objectionable in the office?"

"It's different. The details concerning the airplane can mean life or death." He continued earnestly, trying to make her understand, knowing he failed. "Paperwork in the office drives me crazy—it isn't immediate or . . ."

"But it is, Luke. Can't you see that?" She pushed her fingers through her hair and steadied her voice. "You can't run a business by ignoring the paperwork, not if you expect to be successful."

He studied her sober expression. "It goes further than that," he said slowly, the words emerging with reluctance. "I lose socks. I forget to pay the phone bill and the office utilities." He raised his hands and let them fall.

Sam closed her eyes. "I don't know how you can live like that."

He tossed another log onto the fire.

Reaching into herself, Sam fought hard to be fair. "I imagine you can't comprehend the satisfaction gained from ticking items off a list." She watched him nod and her heart ached. All that was good and fine and strong between them was being eroded by the reality lying beyond the craggy mountain spines.

"Some people see the forest, darlin', and some see the trees," he said softly.

"Without the trees, there is no forest." It wasn't going to work. They would drive each other crazy.

As if he sensed her thoughts, Luke passed a hand over his eyes then stared into the chilly darkness beyond the circle of firelight. Standing, he reached a hand to her. "Let's call it a night, darlin'. Tomorrow's another day. We'll see how things look then."

Sam suspected—no, she *knew*—that everything would be the same. They were poles apart on the important issues. For a brief and wonderful time she had allowed herself to be lulled into thinking love might overcome their differences. But now she wasn't as certain. Love might hold them together for a while, but in the end their basic differences would tear them apart.

Aching inside, she silently followed him into the tent. And when he curled around her, she lay stiffly in the cradle of his arms watching her fingers tighten into a fist. Gently she struck the pine boughs spread beneath them.

"Sam? We'll work this out. I love you."

She sensed the question pride prevented him from asking. But she couldn't tell him that she loved him. The confusion whirling in her mind stopped the words on her tongue.

When his large callused hands gently turned her to face him, she protested feebly. There was too much uneasiness between them to encourage making love.

But when his lips claimed hers, a light shudder of heat rippled over her skin and she felt herself helplessly responding to his growing desire. Whatever else lay between them, there was this also: a wild and urgent physical passion that she could no more deny than she could deny the expectant tension suddenly flaming in the pit of her stomach.

Clinging to him as warm, teasing kisses trailed down her throat, she marveled that Luke Bannister had only to look at her in that special way and she melted inside. Why this should be, she didn't know. She only knew that his vibrant gaze could reach depths within her that no other man had touched. He stirred emotions she didn't fully understand. And when his strong rough fingers stroked her naked skin, a breathless urgency possessed her unlike anything she had ever experienced.

"Oh, Luke. Luke. Hold me," she whispered against his hungry lips. Her voice was a throaty plea. "Hold me and tell me everything will be all right."

"I love you, Sam."

His hands stroked the length of her trembling body, found the zipper to her slacks and slid it down. Then they were both hurriedly pulling off their clothes, shivering in the chill mountain air, holding each other tightly as a flaming moist heat flashed along their bodies to warm them.

Sam slid her hands over the swell of muscle tensing along his shoulders. "I love the feel of you," she whispered helplessly, lost in a tide of sensation. His skin was smooth and hard, unlike the soft, yielding texture of her own body.

Her head pressed backward into the cushioning pine boughs as her body arched to the skilled teasing of his lips, and she felt her nipples burst into bloom beneath the warm circling of his tongue. Cold air nipped at their naked bodies but Sam felt only the fire singing through her veins as his hands curved over her hips and drew her against him.

Not until they were both gasping with urgency did Luke enter her. A sound like a sob tore from Sam's raw throat and she held him fiercely to her heart, kissing him so deeply that her lips felt bruised when she finally pulled away.

"Shhh," Luke soothed, his hands cupping her face.

"I—I—" Their earlier conversation had left her tense with the need for a quick mindless release. She wanted him to take her wildly, with hard powerful strokes; she longed for a stormy coupling that would wash all thought from her mind.

Instead Luke lay quietly above her, his fingers light and gentle as he brushed back her hair. He kissed her softly, thoroughly, as unhurried as if they shared eternity. At first his insistence on tenderness frustrated Sam. Her hands curled into fists on his naked back. Then, as his lips parted hers and his tongue sweetly explored, she relaxed beneath his powerful body and surrendered to the slow, sensual pacing.

The problems she had feared would intrude fled from her mind as her thoughts emptied of all but the pleasurable sensation of his large strong hands stroking her body and the velvety softness of his kisses. Soon, very soon, the world narrowed to Luke's face, to tender blue eyes and a mouth that brushed a tremble of blissful urgency wherever it touched. His hands explored her naked skin as if memorizing every soft curve, each sweet hollow and swell. And her own hands sought and memorized as well, slipping from the hard bulge of his shoulders across the heavy forest on his chest and then dropping to his strength.

Sam closed her dark lashes and lost herself in touching and in being touched, in the long, slow strokes of his body fulfilling her own. And when her eager flesh quivered on the rim of release, Luke quieted, prolonging their joy until neither could bear the rapturous demands of mounting urgency another second. Then they sought each other with a sudden wildness that swept Sam's breath away, that coated her skin with a gleaming sheen of heated perspiration and darkened her gaze nearly to black.

She writhed beneath him, her hair thrashing back and forth across the pine boughs, her fingers clasping to draw him deeper into her. She felt a building ecstasy growing within her, spiraling through her body until she trembled violently in his arms and held him so tightly their hearts beat in unison. At the final lucid moment, she cried out his name and then her body shuddered deeply and convulsively and the joyful splendor of it was almost too blissful to endure.

Later when they had hurriedly dressed, laughing at the cold, and she lay within the warm shelter of his arms, Sam reflected drowsily that she had never felt as totally fulfilled. She hadn't thought it possible. Their lovemaking had possessed a special quality tonight, a tenderness mixed with passion that had led them both to heights they hadn't expected. She blinked into the darkness in wonderment, quietly astonished at the joy her body found in his.

"Luke?" she whispered. "I do love you." But the regular rise and fall of his breath on her cheek confirmed that he was asleep. After a moment, Sam told herself it was just as well. Confusing doubts lay in ambush at the back of her mind, waiting to confuse her. Drawing a breath, Sam firmly pushed aside the negative thoughts. She didn't want anything to spoil the magic they had shared tonight. Not yet. There would be plenty of time to evaluate their relationship after they were rescued.

The helicopters found them in the morning.

Chapter Ten

Sam was first to hear the whickering chop of whirling blades. She scrambled out of the tent and waved frantically.

"Here! We're down here!"

From behind her, she heard a hiss as Luke hastily sprinkled water over the coals in the fire pit. A thin plume of smoke twisted upward past the pines and aspens. Almost immediately two helicopters appeared, swinging in hovering arcs above the tree-tops. They dipped, then lifted and disappeared behind the foliage.

"They've seen us," Luke said, shading his eyes. "As soon as they find a place to land, we're rescued."

Sam stared at the crisp autumn sky, listening to the unnatural whirring against the frosty stillness of the morning.

It was over, truly over. Their dreamlike capsule of timelessness had opened to admit the world. She felt like shouting with relief, but the same instant, tears of loss pricked her eyelids. Confusion darkened her gaze and trembled along the curve of her uncertain smile.

Luke stared into her troubled eyes, then his arms circled her waist and gently he drew her against his chest and rested his chin atop her hair. Sam leaned into him, feeling his solid warmth against her cheek, his broad chest beneath her fingertips, his thighs hard against her own. Blinking, she inhaled the good male scent of him, Luke's scent, and she tried to sort through a whirl of conflicting emotions. The task was hopeless.

Standing before their makeshift tent, they held each other and waited. And when they heard the shouts and noise of men crashing through the brush, Luke breathed her name against her hair and Sam released a long, slow breath. They stepped apart, still holding hands, and looked at each other.

"I don't want it to end," Sam whispered, staring up into his vivid gaze. "Isn't that silly? Something in me doesn't want to be rescued."

He stroked her cheek. "I know."

They gazed deeply into each other's eyes, asking silent questions and receiving answers they couldn't read.

"Here they are! Over here!"

In an instant the small clearing was overrun by men wearing khaki pants and shirts. A half-dozen voices surrounded them, all speaking at once. Someone asked if a stretcher was required; another voice shouted, "Negative." A man with a jug-sized thermos offered hot coffee and asked if they wanted cigarettes. Both Sam and Luke accepted the coffee gratefully, then did what they could to answer the questions raining over them.

After Luke had sketched a broad outline of the crash and their long hike, one of the helicopter pilots thrust out his hand. "I want to shake your hand, man." He grinned broadly, admiration lighting a boyish face. "I saw that Fairchild. You must have had an angel on your shoulder when you landed that one."

Luke winked at Sam. "I had an angel with me, that's for sure."

"I'd have bet a year's pay that nobody walked away from that crash. We flat couldn't believe it when we saw the arrow and found your note."

Sam gazed at Luke, her eyes shining with quiet pride. "No one but Luke Bannister could have landed that plane."

"I believe it," the pilot agreed enthusiastically.

"Maybe," Luke said slowly, his modesty surprising Sam. "But a good pilot wouldn't have crashed it in the first place. And if I'd had the sense to file a flight plan"—he cast Sam a rueful smile—"it would have been a lot easier for you boys."

The copter pilot grinned. "That's for damned sure. But it happens all the time. You know that." His boyish grin widened. "You two look like hell."

Surprised, they turned to examine each other. Then smiles curved their sunburned lips as they saw each other as the pilot saw them.

A ring of fading yellow and purple underlined Luke's eye, his new beard was straggly and uneven. An insect bite had swollen his cheek; bruises showed along his forearms and where his collar opened at his throat. Even so, Sam decided he was easily the handsomest man she'd ever seen.

As for herself, her hair swung limp and tangled against her shoulders. Flakes of sunburned skin peeled from her brow, nose, and cheeks. Her clothing was torn and dirty. A violet weariness circled her eyes; bruises marked exposed skin. She limped from the blisters stinging her heels. She and Luke were both pale and tired.

The copter pilot's glance flicked over Sam's full breasts and slim hips then arched toward Bannister. "Even so, I envy you, man." He watched his men pull down the small tent and fold it. Khaki-clad men dismantled the campsite, leaving the environment clean. Then he returned his grin to Luke. His suggestive smile sobered when he gazed into the hard pinpoints of Luke's stare.

"Would you like to step into the forest and discuss

the matter further?" Luke asked, his growl danger-
ously soft, his stare unwavering.

The pilot hastily raised his palms and edged backward. "Hey, man, I didn't mean any offense."

"Tell it to the lady."

The pilot stared into Luke's steely expression then
swung toward Sam. "I apologize, Miss Adams. I
didn't intend . . ."

"I accept your apology," Sam responded quietly. A
deep pink had appeared beneath her rosy sunburn.
Raising her head, she gazed gratefully into Luke's
eyes. Luke slipped a strong arm around her waist
and together they walked to the waiting helicopter
and climbed inside.

Within minutes, the pilot, Mike Cabot, had raised
the helicopter above the pines. Had the campfire not
continued to smoke, Sam couldn't have identified
their campsite or the men still working below, so
quickly did everything vanish beneath the sea of
autumn foliage. The helicopter soared upward into a
wide expanse of cloudless blue; the treetops rapidly
dropped beneath them.

Luke leaned near her ear, and his broad, tanned
hand clasped hers reassuringly. "Frightened?"

Biting her lip, Sam dared a glance at the winking
red and blue lights outside the window, then she
shook her head. "No," she lied. She tried to tell herself that the worst had happened and she'd survived.
But it didn't help. She was never going to enjoy
flying.

Cabot spoke into the microphone attached to his
headset. "We've got them. They're a little the worse
for wear, but no serious injuries." He listened a
moment, nodding automatically. "Okay. Then we'll
bypass Leadville and bring them on in to Denver."
Again he nodded. "St. Anthony's Hospital. Got it."

"A hospital?" Sam asked, her eyes wide.

"Standard procedure." Luke squeezed her hand.

The touch of his strong fingers anchored her physically, but her mind had numbed before the flurry of men and activity. She didn't think she required a doctor's attention, but she was too weary to protest. It was easier to drift with the flow.

As the whining roar of the blades and the engine made conversation difficult, Sam leaned to the window, finding it impossible to comprehend that she had walked those spiny ridges and plunging valleys slipping past below. But her feet believed it, she thought wryly. The heels on her shoes were worn to nubs. Now that she no longer faced another day of walking, she allowed herself to feel the full pain of broken blisters.

"Sam?" Luke's hands slid up her arms, turning her to face him. "I love you." Tired blue eyes searched her face, and she knew he was more exhausted than he'd let on. "And we're going to be married. Nothing else is important."

"Oh, Luke." She stared into the strong planes and angles of his bearded face, responding to the intensity flickering in his vibrant blue eyes. "I love you, too," she answered quietly. "Right this minute, I love you." Dropping her head, she glanced at the terrain sliding past below. The real world flew toward them. And the things he dismissed as unimportant rushed into her mind.

He must have sensed her thoughts as his grasp tightened around her fingers until she winced. "Give us a chance, Sam. That's all I ask. Just give me a chance to convince you how right we are together."

Were they? She'd thought so when they faced the wilderness together. But now she wasn't so certain. He said he loved her, but he was also the man who had said, "I'll put you out of business." In the real world they were adversaries.

Mike Cabot called back over his shoulder. "We'll be landing on top of St. Anthony's in about five minutes." The city had appeared beneath them, a neat grid of intersecting lines and autumn colors. "I'm afraid you're going to be besieged by the media. Are you up to it?"

"Darlin'?"

"We might as well get it over with." She mustered a smile. "A person who's eaten grasshoppers can face anything."

They were surrounded before the helicopter blades had ceased spinning. The instant they stepped to the rooftop, a crush of people rushed forward, shouting questions. A waiting doctor and two nurses attempted valiantly to intercede, then hastened into the building in search of reinforcements.

Sam blinked at the exploding flashbulbs and tried to hear the questions in the rising babble. Stepping backward from the forest of microphones, she unconsciously sought Luke's sheltering arm, uniting with his strength and calm forbearance. The media people jammed the rooftop, blocking the emergency landing pads.

"How did the crash occur?"

"What did you do for food?"

"Did you have a map? Where did you sleep?"

It was chaos. Sam stared at the blur of faces pressing around them, feeling like prey. She wondered uneasily if the media would have been so relentless if she or Luke were injured. Would they have followed a stretcher, microphones extended?

Smiling, Luke raised a hand and shouted for silence. When he had their attention, he spoke. "We're both tired and hungry, and I'm sure the hospital doesn't want us obstructing the rooftop. We'll give you five minutes, then let's call it a day." He pointed to a slender blond woman from Channel Nine. "How about you asking questions for everyone."

A groan of protest arose, then settled into a rustling quiet as the woman from Channel Nine triumphantly began her interview. The others scribbled notes.

In response to her questions, Luke explained the mountain squall and briefly detailed the crash.

"Were you frightened, Miss Adams?"

The question struck Sam as utterly ridiculous and she suspected her strained smile revealed as much. "I was terrified. But Luke—Mr. Bannister—was wonderful. Without his expertise, we wouldn't have . . ."

The reporter cut her off. "Is it true, Mr. Bannister, that you didn't file a flight plan?"

"All too true." Luke's lopsided, Clark Gable grin flashed engagingly. Sam noticed an unmistakable gleam of interest in the reporter's eye. "That's an error I won't make again."

The reporter wet her lips and pushed back a shining wave of blond hair. "Which of you decided to walk out of the mountains?"

"It was a joint decision," Luke answered, his arm tightening around Sam's shoulders. "Miss Adams contributed equally toward our survival. Without her suggestions, we . . ."

The reporter's gaze swept Luke's broad shoulders. "How did you protect yourselves from the cold nights?"

"We had a tent and . . ."

"How large a tent?"

Sam didn't like the suggestive tone of the woman's voice or the knowing, almost envious, gleam in her eyes. "Luke made a tent from a length of tarp."

"You slept together in the tent?" the woman purred.

Sam's face tightened. "I think this interview has concluded."

Luke nodded. Pushing the microphones aside, he guided Sam through the throng of protests toward a door through which the doctor was emerging. The security guards behind him quickly formed a barrier, allowing only Sam and Luke to slip through.

Inside, Dr. McCullough introduced himself, then led them toward a bank of elevators, smiling thinly. "You two are big news. You've made the front pages for the past two days."

Sam looked past his glasses into concerned dark eyes. "Do our families know we're safe?"

Nodding, McCullough pressed her fingers. "We've notified Mr. Bannister's family, and your parents are waiting downstairs." His gaze scanned her sunburn with professional interest. She noticed his fingers had slid to her wrist as he measured her pulse rate.

The nurse at Luke's side scanned his eye then lifted his wrist, staring at her watch. Sam wet her lips and returned Luke's encouraging smile. Her head still whirled from the reporter's demands; she'd never felt as exhausted in her life. Her knees were weak and rubbery.

Luke's wide lips framed a silent, "I love you," then the elevator doors whooshed open and McCullough guided Sam into a softly green corridor. The doors closed and Luke was gone.

The next hours passed in a blur. Sam vaguely recalled her parents' tearful hugs and embraces, then she was led away and given a thorough physical examination. She remembered insisting on a shower and a shampoo. A variety of faces appeared with trays of equipment and bottles. Someone gave her a plastic container and pushed her gently into the small bathroom off her room; someone else wrapped a dark cuff around her arm and withdrew a blood sample. A cool disk slipped beneath her cotton gown and pressed against her heart. An IV tube snaked up from her wrist to a drip bottle suspended from a metal frame.

She remembered asking repeatedly for Luke, then her damp head settled against the crisp white hospital pillow and her leaden eyes slowly closed. Drowsily, she commanded herself to sit up and call the office, but her body wouldn't obey. In two minutes she was asleep.

She slept for fifteen hours. When she awoke, Natalie Adams was knitting in a chair beside her bed and Frank Adams was sipping coffee at the window. Sam pulled herself to a sitting position and blinked at her parents with affection.

"Don't you two have anything better to do than hang around hospitals?" she smiled.

For the next two hours, she answered questions and then eagerly devoured the lunch tray delivered by a smiling nurse. When she finished eating, she leaned back against mounded pillows and savored a second cup of hot black coffee.

While Natalie Adams answered the constantly ringing phone, taking messages from friends and well-wishers, Sam visited with her father.

She drew a breath and looked into the depths of her cup. "We lost the Chilton account, Dad."

Frank Adams patted her hand. "You knew you'd lose a few, honey." His weathered face pleated into a reassuring expression. "You're doing a fine job."

Sam gazed at him thoughtfully. Naturally, he wouldn't let her see his disappointment. Especially not when she was lying in a hospital bed. She suppressed a sigh and finished her coffee.

"Sam, honey. You don't have to explain what happens with every account. You know that, don't you?"

Sam nodded slowly. But the truth was that she did feel compelled to explain. Her father had built Adams Air from nothing into a respected company known for dependability and service. She'd never believe that he wasn't interested in what happened to the business under her stewardship.

"Honey, Adams Air is yours now." Her father smiled, a comfortable, reassuring smile. "At least you haven't missed a payment yet. And you can do with it whatever you want. Hell, I don't care. Sell it, give it to the Salvation Army, close the doors and walk away. Whatever you want to do, Sam, it's your decision."

What she desperately wanted was to succeed. She didn't know how great a portion of her parents' retirement income depended on her buy-out, but she suspected the amount was considerable. She had to succeed for their sake as well as for her own. Most important, she wanted to be worthy of the pride she saw in her father's eyes. Dropping her head backward on the pillows, she stared at the ceiling. Her major stumbling block was Luke Bannister.

Luke. That she could even think of him as a stumbling block revived her previous doubts. Several serious problems lay between herself and Luke Bannister. The quickest solution to Luke's problems would be to merge the two companies. After all, she was *his* major obstacle to success. But would a merger resolve her concerns? Would it lay her doubts to rest? Would a merger truly be beneficial for Adams Air?

"Your mother and I are very proud of what you've

accomplished, Sam." Her father's dark eyes softened.
"Don't be so hard on yourself, honey."

"Oh, Dad." Sam pushed an impatient hand
through her hair. "I haven't done anything expect
patch here and patch there and try to hold everything together."

"But you've done it, haven't you?"

"Maybe. But Luke . . ." She bit off the words. How
could she complain about Luke stealing her business
when Luke was the man she loved? When Luke had
saved her life?

Frank Adams' eyes lit at the mention of Bannister's name. "When I saw that plane and read your
note . . ." He shook his head, remembering. "I figured
Luke Bannister had to be the best damned pilot in
the region."

"He's . . . special." Naturally, Frank Adams had
inspected the crash site. Nothing could have kept
him away. Sam exchanged a smile with her mother,
then Natalie Adams tilted her white head, judging
Sam's tone.

"How special is he, dear?" she asked, a twinkle in
her eyes. "Is he as dashing as the papers make him
out to be?"

Sam had seen the papers earlier. They showed
Luke sitting in an open cockpit of a navy fighter
plane and somehow the reporters had dug up a photo
of herself wearing a clinging white bathing suit. The
media was playing up the romantic aspects of two
rivals stranded in the wilderness.

"Judge for yourself," Sam replied with a smile as
Luke loomed in the doorway of her room, red roses
spilling from his arms.

He'd shaved his beard and had found time for a
haircut. And he wore new Levi's and a crew-necked
sweater that matched the vivid blue of his eyes. A
glow of heat swept through Sam's body. Helplessly,

she looked at his large hands holding the delicate roses and remembered his touch on her nakedness, alternately gentle then rough with desire. She bit her lip and swallowed, then she spoke in a shaky voice, "Luke Bannister, please meet my parents, Frank and Natalie Adams."

Luke gave Natalie a broad smile then thrust out his hand and returned Frank Adams' firm handclasp. Sam decided he looked like Clark Gable more than ever. A sidelong glance toward her mother confimed that Natalie had immediately noted the uncanny resemblance.

"I'm pleased to meet you, sir." Luke met Frank Adams' appraisal with a direct look. "Did Sam tell you that we're going to be married?"

Sam rolled her eyes and smiled. She might have known.

"Samantha!" Natalie dropped her knitting and ignored the ringing phone, her eyes widening in delight. "Is this true? You're finally getting married?"

"Yes, ma'am, she is." Luke smiled at Sam's mother. "I see where Sam gets her beautiful eyes."

Natalie's cheeks pinked with pleasure, but Frank Adams was not as easy a conquest. He continued to grip Luke's hand, his eyes cool and expressionless.

"The papers say you're ex-navy. Is that right?"

Luke nodded.

"You navy pilots don't know crap from crayolas about flying," Frank Adams challenged. "Why should I let you marry my daughter?"

Luke's eyes cooled. He leaned forward until he was nearly nose to nose with Sam's father. "I'm telling you that I'm going to marry your daughter, sir—I'm not asking your permission. And I'd like to see one of you sissy air force pilots land on a carrier in high seas. Some say if there's a cloud in the sky, the air force won't fly."

They stared hard into each other's eyes, then both broke into wide grins. Frank Adams clapped Luke on the shoulder and beamed at his wife and daughter. "I like him, even if he is navy. He's got grit."

Sam smiled in amazement. Frank had never approved of any man she'd brought home. None had been good enough for his little girl.

Luke handed Natalie the roses, then he bent over Sam's bed and kissed her. The instant his lips touched hers, Sam felt the familiar warm weakness spread through her body as flesh and bones melted at his touch. An embarrassed pink glowed radiantly across her cheeks as she pushed him away with a tiny nod toward her watching parents. "Is there anyone you can't charm?" she whispered against his warm mouth.

"I'm irresistible," he laughed. Then his gaze followed the tube leading from her wrist to the drip bottle and his eyes sobered. "How are you feeling?"

"All this is just for show." Sam smiled. "Dr. McCullough says I can go home tomorrow. How about you?" He looked vibrantly alive, as if nothing they'd experienced had actually occurred. The only reminder of what the papers had termed their "ordeal" was a faint, dark smudge beneath his eye.

"Discharged this morning." His eyes caressed her oval face then lingered on the front of her shapeless hospital gown. "Remind me to buy you a dozen gowns just like that one. You look gorgeous."

Sam grinned. "Liar." Her mother had brought lipstick and mascara, and a ribbon to tie back her hair. But her face was still a raw sheet of sunburned skin. And the gown was a hopeless sack. She smiled into his soft gaze and thought of a black silk nightgown hanging in her closet at home. Her dark eyes danced with a teasing promise.

"So." Frank Adams cleared his throat, reminding them that they had an audience. "My little girl is going to be married."

"Yes, sir," Luke answered. "Someone has to make an honest woman of her."

"Luke!"

Luke's eyes widened into circles of innocence. "It seems the newspapers are convinced that hiking out of the mountains is tantamount to a romantic tryst. Therefore, I'm honor-bound to do what I can to salvage the lady's reputation." He shrugged with a gesture of exaggerated helplessness, the motion so foreign as to be ridiculous. "The last thing I want to do is marry an ugly girl like Sam, sir, but I don't know what else to do. Besides, she begged me."

"*I* begged *you*?" Sam sputtered.

"It was pitiful, sir. I'm glad you weren't there to see it. Begging and pleading and carrying on like . . ."

Frank Adams burst into laughter and suddenly everyone was talking at once, trying to be heard over the constant ringing of the telephone. Then Sam's father drew Luke to the window and Sam overheard snatches of conversation regarding freight limits and scheduling and what she thought of as "plane talk." At her bedside, Natalie eagerly discussed caterers and gowns and guest lists. When Natalie paused to answer the telephone, Sam bit her lip and stared uncertainly at Luke Bannister.

He was startlingly handsome. Sunlight streamed in the window, falling softly across his black curls. The blue sweater pulled across his shoulders as he crossed his arms over his chest, defining a swell of heavy muscle. As she watched, he threw back his head and laughed, snowy teeth flashing against bronzed skin. He was in his element, swapping stories and telling tales. Sam studied his confident stance, listened to a rumble of laughter and felt a rush of heat sing through her veins.

When she looked at him, her doubts seemed to evaporate. Oh, Luke, she thought frantically, stay with me. Don't leave me alone for a minute.

A nurse bustled inside the room, interrupting Sam's silent plea, and placed a dinner tray on the bedside table. Frank kissed her brow and squeezed her fingers. "If you don't mind, honey, I think I'll take Luke out to the field and show off our planes before it gets dark."

"Of course I don't mind." Her voice emerged with an odd sound and she wondered if she did mind.

Luke's lips brushed hers and his large hand looped a dark lock of hair back from her cheek. "I'll be back later tonight, darlin'."

"If I know Dad, he'll take you out to the field, then he'll want to stop for dinner and a drink or two to talk airplanes." She touched her finger to his lips. "I suspect you won't be back until late."

"Do you mind?"

"You bet I mind. I wish I could go with you both." She smothered an exaggerated yawn. "But I think I'll be asleep two minutes after I eat this feast."

"Some feast. Mystery roast and mashed air. Want me to bring you some grasshoppers for breakfast? Now that's a feast."

"No thanks, I'm trying to quit." Sam smiled up at him.

"All right, then. I'll pick you up in the morning." He squeezed her hand and kissed her again, then she watched her father drape an arm over Luke's shoulder and they sauntered out the door, head to head, deep in conversation. Sam envied them both.

Sam stared at the door, suddenly feeling as tired

as she'd claimed. The room seemed terribly empty without Luke in it.

Natalie smiled happily. "He's very nice, Samantha. Your father likes him."

Sam murmured an absent response. She poked at a fluffy mound of potatoes. What was the matter with her? She should be elated that Luke had favorably impressed her parents. Thinking hard, she attempted to isolate her emotions, but failed.

Natalie eyed her daughter shrewdly, measuring the silence. "Is something wrong, Samantha? Is this happening too fast?"

"I don't know." Sam pushed away the dinner tray with a faint sound of exasperation. "One minute I think . . . and then the next minute he . . ." She lifted her hands and watched them fall, annoyed with herself for sounding indecisive and confused.

"Give it a little time, honey. You don't know each other very well. If it's right, it will stand the test of time. There's no need to rush into anything."

Sam gazed at her mother with gratitude moistening her dark eyes. She knew how much Natalie Adams wanted a grandchild. "I think we know each other pretty well," she said slowly. "Sometimes you can know someone for years without really understanding them. And other times you can meet someone and five minutes later you know them as if they've always been part of your life." She sighed and transferred her gaze to the window. "I think Luke and I know each other very well. Maybe that's the problem."

Natalie considered for a moment. "No one's perfect, honey," she said gently.

Later, when Sam had convinced her mother to go home and get some rest, she replayed their conversation in her mind. Is that what I'm doing, she thought, expecting Luke to be perfect? She resisted the idea.

No, she didn't expect him to be perfect, but she did expect him to be competent. And no competent businessman overlooked an item as crucially important as insurance. And she expected him to be honest about his motivations and ambitions. Her troubled eyes stared at nothing as she reviewed their shifting relationship.

When the phone rang, she gazed at it a moment then stretched out her hand. "Hello?" When she realized she'd barked the word, she drew a slow breath then tried again, her voice softer this time.

"Hi, boss lady." Marva's voice boomed over the wires, as sturdy and vivacious as Marva herself. "How were things in the wilderness? How are you feeling and why didn't you tell me Bannister was so great-looking? I'd like to be marooned with him myself . . ."

Gradually, Sam relaxed as Marva prattled on, her conversation a mixture of questions and comments and good-natured opinions. When Marva paused for breath, Sam asked, "Are you still at the office?"

"No rest for the wicked," Marva confirmed cheerfully.

"I'm not paying you enough." Sam laughed as Marva heartily agreed, then her expression sobered. "Any disasters I should know about?"

"When you hear, you'll wish you'd never been rescued."

Sam rested her forehead against her palm and closed her eyes. "That bad?"

"I've got a stack of bills here from creditors who are probably wild with joy that you're alive and well. Want me to go through them?"

Sam nodded. "Shoot." She listened carefully and scribbled a page of hurried notes. "Anything else?"

"I'm just getting started. Dr. Belowski says Marvin Crewes can't fly again until his blood pressure comes down, which leaves us without a pilot for the Cheyenne run. But that's okay because we don't have a plane either. One of the DC-6's is leaking oil like a sieve and had to be pulled for an overhaul. I'm stalling the Cheyenne accounts until you get back." Marva paused and Sam heard the rustle of shuffling paper. "Ellis McCarther ran into some weather between here and Boise and three crates of baby chickens broke open. As of an hour ago, there were baby chickens all over the plane and all over the Boise runway. And they aren't potty-trained. Ever try to chase down a baby chicken in the dark? There's a lot of slipping and sliding going on up there."

Sam's smile faded as Marva continued.

"Stonemount Tires called three times yesterday and twice today. And Rocky Mountain Frozen Foods isn't going to renew their contract. Mr. Weston said he got a better rate from Bannister Air Freight. Sam? Are you there, Sam?"

The real world crashed over her like a bucket of icy water.

Chapter Eleven

❦

"Very nice," Luke said. "I like it." He stood in the center of Sam's spacious living room as Sam quickly glanced through an accumulation of mail, then fed her goldfish while she waited for the coffee to finish perking.

"Thank you." His compliments raised a flush of pleasure to her cheeks. "I like it too." After she'd opened the french doors leading to a flagstone patio, Sam turned back toward the living room.

She tried to see her home as Luke was seeing it. All in all, she decided she was pleased with the ambience she had created. Warm earth tones opened before her, a deep-piled rust carpet, glowing wood paneling, a sofa and chairs in bright autumn gold. And her pride and joy, a moss-rock fireplace flanked on either side by bookcases displaying well-read favorites and objects she had collected over the years: a porcelain figure she'd purchased in Spain, her grandmother's brass candlesticks, a tiny wooden rocker she'd watched a Vail artist carve . . .

Luke leaned to inspect a painting one of Sam's friends had done, a cornucopia spilling squash, pumpkins, and autumn corn. "Your home is warm, intimate, very much Sam Adams." He nodded to himself. "I can just picture you curled up on the sofa on a cold, snowy night with a fire crackling and a stack of Willie Nelson recordings on the stereo."

Sam had spent many such evenings. Smiling, she stepped into her small neat kitchen and poured two mugs of coffee, sliding Luke's across the counter of the pass-through connecting her kitchen and living room.

They faced each other across the counter and Sam was glad the pass-through separated them. When she gazed into Luke's vivid blue eyes her stomach tightened suggestively and all rational thought fled her mind. It would have been so easy to simply walk into his arms and give in to the tingling demands racing along her nerve endings. She gave herself a small shake and an amused reminder that it was only ten o'clock in the morning. A little early for the type of thoughts heating her mind.

"Why are you hiding in the kitchen?" Luke teased. "Afraid to come out here and sit beside me?" A meandering breeze lightly billowed the draperies framing the patio doors and ruffled Luke's black curls.

Sam smiled and hooked a soft wave of brown hair behind her ear. "You bet I'm afraid of you. Sitting next to you does peculiar things to me. Right now I'd rather talk."

Luke's narrowed gaze scanned the soft swell of breasts hinted beneath her opened collar, then he heaved an exaggerated sigh. "There are things I'd rather do. But if you insist on talking, we'll talk. We have a lot of plans to make."

"Luke . . ."

"And a lot of loose ends to tie." He tasted his coffee. "I'm meeting my insurance agent in about an hour. Unless he asks me to stay in Denver, I'll return to Aspen tomorrow morning." He rolled his eyes toward the beamed ceiling. "God only knows what shape my office is in by now." He looked at her across the countertop. "Are you going in today?"

Sam nodded. "Marva's done a terrific job, but several problems arose that's she's saving for me. It's going to be a busy week." She drew a breath. "Marva tells me that we lost another account to Bannister Air."

"Oh?"

"Does the name Rocky Mountain Frozen Foods mean anything to you, sir?" Sam tried to keep her tone light and uncaring. And knew she failed.

"Stan Weston. Ex-navy." Luke drained his coffee and placed the mug on the counter. "A good man."

"I always thought so." Reaching out a hand, Sam straightened the cover over the toaster. A place for everything and everything in its place. "Are you planning to steal any more of my clients?"

"Nope. We're working together now, remember?" He slid from the stool and glanced at his watch. "I'll be late if I don't leave this minute. Dinner tonight?"

Sam stared at him, experiencing the same mix of panic and frustration she'd felt over the Chilton deal. Then she looked into his vibrant smile and her resistance crumbled. She nodded and walked around to the living room, closing her eyes for a brief moment as his arm circled her slim waist.

"We'll go somewhere wildly extravagant. We have a lot to celebrate." He smiled at her quick glance toward his jeans and sweater. "Don't worry, I'll scare up a suit and tie."

Thinking about Rocky Mountain Frozen Foods didn't exactly put Sam in a celebrating mood. She suspected an afternoon at her office wasn't going to improve her frame of mind. "Are you sure you wouldn't rather make it a simple evening? Something takeout? Maybe a pizza?"

Luke grinned down at her as he gathered her into his arms. "Are you suffering pasta withdrawal?"

"Something like that." She inhaled deeply, sampling the light after-shave lingering on his cheeks, trying to ignore the leap of excitement she'd felt the instant his arms surrounded her. Damn. Her intellect warned her to step back, to maintain a distance, but her traitorous body leaned against him eagerly.

Luke's large hands ran up her arms, raising a light shiver in their path. "No, darlin', no pizza tonight. If I can get last-minute reservations, we'll go to the Chateau Pyrenees."

"The Chateau?" Sam tilted her head back and blinked up at him. "That's terribly expensive, Luke."

He smiled. "It's only money, darlin'. Tonight is special—we're celebrating life and love."

Both brimmed in his eyes as he gazed down at her. And then his wide, warm lips descended to cover hers and suddenly everything seemed right and reasonable. Sam's arms circled his neck and her body melted against him, fitting perfectly into his hard angles.

"Sam . . ." he murmured huskily, his voice muffled in her hair.

She laughed softly and pushed him toward the door. "You're late, remember?" Her own voice was throaty with desire. She felt a wistful pang of disappointment as Luke glanced at his watch and ruefully admitted she was correct. He gave her a jaunty salute, then closed the door behind him.

Sam rinsed his mug and placed it in the dishwasher, then carried a second cup of coffee onto the patio, inhaling deeply and hoping the cold October breeze would blow the cobwebs from her mind.

Instead, her gaze settled on the distant spines of the mountains, a jagged sweep across the clear, crisp blue of the western horizon. She wished her thoughts were as sharply defined. She wished she didn't feel the uneasy edge of uncertainty at the back of her mind. But she did.

Sighing, she locked the patio doors, straightened the kitchen, then collected her car keys, purse, and jacket. After all, she assured herself, she didn't have to decide anything right this minute. There was plenty of time.

The mound of papers overflowing Sam's desk was as overwhelming as she had feared. The telephone rang constantly.

"Marva, would you put the phone on automatic answer and come in here, please?" After hanging her jacket in the closet, Sam poured a cup of coffee and frowned at her desktop. An office supply salesman waited in the lobby to see her; a quick glance at her calendar confirmed she was to meet with a representative from Piedmont Air Lines later this afternoon. She'd hoped to purchase a plane Piedmont was phasing out, one which could be refitted as a cargo liner.

Sam had made the appointment in a burst of optimism several weeks ago. Now she wondered at the wisdom of purchasing additional equipment. Her profits had shrunk alarmingly over the past several weeks.

Sighing, she seated herself behind her desk, chatted a minute with Marva, then cleared a space among the papers and began dictating instructions and replies. After two hours, Marva pleaded for mercy and Sam released her to the phones and typewriter. Sam canceled her appointment with the Piedmont representative, poured more coffee, and tackled a second stack of invoices, bills of lading, memos, and order forms. The work progressed slowly, constantly interrupted by Marva's questions or phone calls that wouldn't wait.

Marva popped her head in the door. "Captain James is here to see you."

"Not today," Sam groaned, making a face. Harry James was her chief pilot and a pain in the neck. Captain James had made it abundantly clear that,

in his opinion, women should be nurses or steward-
esses, not doctors or pilots, or company presidents.
Harry usually wore a lapel pin featuring a large
scarlet C.P., standing for Chauvinist Pig. He was
proud of it.

Marva grinned and lowered her voice. "He's right
outside."

"Okay," Sam sighed, pushing at her hair. "Send
him in."

Harry started talking before he reached her desk,
his face thunderous as usual. "What's this
horsesh—uh, crap about grounding Marvin Crewes?
And why has that woman pulled *Louise* out of
schedule?"

Sam folded her hands on her desk, staring point-
edly at the cap he didn't remove. "That woman" was
Marva, but she hadn't the faintest idea who Louise
might be.

Harry James stared at her, then answered her
question in a tone overflowing with exasperation.
"*Louise* is a perfectly fit DC-6." His expression indicated that he thought any person worth their
paycheck would have known that.

A slight flush pinked Sam's cheeks. She shuffled
through a stack of papers then asked Captain James
if the serial number she read was the plane in
question.

"How the hell would I know the serial number?
Louise is *Louise*. And I want her back in service."

Sam deliberately held her temper in check. "No
plane in the Adams Air fleet leaves the hangar until
the head mechanic says so. And the same principle
applies to Marvin Crewes. Until Dr. Belowski con-
firms that his blood pressure is down, Captain
Crewes is grounded. Those are the rules, Harry."

"Look, Miss Adams, I don't think you understand

what's involved here. Marv wants to fly and we need him."

The color intensified in Sam's face. "I think I understand the freight business quite well, Captain James. Adams Air will not risk a client's cargo to a plane with a marginal safety factor, nor will we entrust it to the judgment of a high-risk pilot. Do I make myself clear?"

"That's one hell of a shortsighted way to run a cargo line. Frank wouldn't have been so damned muleheaded!"

Their eyes clashed and held across the desktop. "If that's how you feel, Captain, then perhaps Adams Air is no longer the best place for you." Sam drew a breath and calmed the sharpness in her tone. "You're sixty-three, Harry. Maybe you'd be happier if you took early retirement."

"Maybe I will, little lady, maybe I just will," he snapped.

Captain James's tone and expression suggested that he believed Adams Air would collapse without his supervision. Suppressing a sigh, Sam stood, signaling the interview had concluded. "Think about it, Harry." She watched him storm from her office, then sank back behind her desk.

In truth, she didn't know how she would manage without Harry James, as irascible as he was. Harry acted as a buffer between Sam and her pilots. Although he made her furious by interpreting her directives to suit himself and simply ignoring instructions he didn't agree with, Harry kept the freight moving smoothly. There was always a pilot available when Sam needed one even when she scheduled a last-minute run or had to add an extra section.

Still, Harry wasn't good for morale. Sam knew she was the butt of many jokes in the crew lounge. She'd seen a crude cartoon tacked to the bulletin board showing a quaking woman being pushed aboard a plane. Sighing, she returned to her paperwork. She'd have to do something about Harry soon. But first, she needed to get Adams Air firmly on its feet. Pushing him out of her mind, she tackled the mess on her desk.

At the end of the day, she still hadn't found time to post her accounts or to assess the damage caused by the loss of Rocky Mountain Frozen Foods and Chilton's business. Sam glanced at her watch and thrust her fingers through her hair. She could work on her ledger—or she could call it a day and go home to a leisurely preparation for tonight's dinner with Luke. Biting her lip, she considered briefly, then pulled a sheaf of papers over the top of the ledger.

"It's after five, boss," Marva announced. She eased her ample figure into the chair across from Sam and lit a cigarette with a sigh of pleasure.

"I thought you'd quit smoking," Sam smiled.

"I did. Then last week happened and I started again." She eyed Sam critically. "You look tired."

"Nothing a hot tub and a little makeup can't repair."

"Seriously, how are you feeling?"

"Like I've been run over by a truck." Sam stretched and leaned backward in her chair. This was the time of day she most enjoyed. By unspoken agreement, she and Marva had long ago fallen into the habit of sharing twenty minutes at the end of the day, relaxing before they hurled themselves into the rush-hour traffic.

"Can you go home and collapse? Or do you have other plans?"

Sam picked up a pencil and turned it between her fingers. "I have other plans."

"I rather thought you might," Marva laughed. "That man's crazy about you, you know."

Sam glanced up in surprise. "How can you say that? You haven't even met him."

"I saw you both on TV last night." Marva's generous mouth curved in a smile. "If I was twenty years younger and twenty pounds lighter, I'd chase that man down and jump on him. Every woman dreams of having a man look at her the way Luke Bannister was looking at you."

"That's how Bill looks at you," Sam said. Marva and Bill Howard enjoyed a marriage much like Sam's parents'—warm and easy and enduring. She suddenly wondered how this was accomplished, how people swept aside individual differences to succeed at something as complicated as marriage. Maybe marriage was a dying art, one that would vanish with her parents' generation. The thought saddened her.

"Bill who?" Marva asked, and they both laughed. After sneaking a peek at her watch, Marva stood. "Time to do battle with the other weary workers." Tactfully, she refrained from voicing the questions she was clearly itching to ask. "See you at dawn, boss."

"Dawn?" Sam grinned. "What kind of slave driver do you work for? Tell her I said nine o'clock is early enough." Rising from her desk, she snapped off the lights and walked to the parking lot with Marva.

The ledger would keep until tomorrow. If she worked on it now, she knew she'd only get depressed. And she didn't want that to happen, not tonight. The fatigue drained from her step as her thoughts jumped ahead and she eagerly anticipated the evening with Luke.

Chapter Twelve

Sam wound her shining hair into a cluster of curls high atop her crown, a style she liked but seldom wore as she'd always thought it made her appear taller. One of the nice things about Luke Bannister was that she could wear her hair up and could choose her highest heels and he would still be taller. Silly as it was, the realization made her feel dainty and ultrafeminine.

Amused at herself, she slid open a mirrored closet door and, after a moment's thought, selected a clinging white jersey that molded her figure before dropping into a soft swirl around her knees. A deceptively modest neckline swept over her shoulders, then plunged to her waist, leaving her back seductively bare. She hooked a rose-colored satin belt around her slender waist, then slipped her feet into rose-colored, high-heeled sandals. After clasping a chain of pearls around her throat, she examined the results in the mirror, surprised by a nervous flutter in her stomach.

She couldn't remember when she'd dressed this carefully for a dinner date. Nor could she recall with any clarity the men who had drifted in and out of her busy life without leaving a lasting impression. None had possessed that certain magical quality that Luke had.

Her fingers reached for a crystal decanter of Chanel Number Five, then she paused and smiled, remembering the fog of scent when Luke had doused her wound. She passed over the Chanel and selected Joy instead, deciding she'd experienced enough Chanel Number Five to last a lifetime. After clipping pearl earrings in place, she stepped back and again inspected herself in the mirror.

Her brown eyes were still too widely spaced, her mouth still too generously wide to match her idea of true beauty. But somehow tonight it didn't matter. She looked stunning. The remainder of her sunburn glowed through her makeup, imparting a healthy radiance. Her hair was elegant and shining. The white jersey molded her breasts like a second skin and swirled about her long legs when she moved. Sam smiled with pleasure, deciding she would do.

After filling the ice bucket, she set out a tray of hors d'oeuvres, then turned on the stereo. She was contemplating building a fire in the fireplace when the doorbell rang.

Sam smoothed her hands over her hips. "You're behaving like a teenager on a first date," she chided herself. Then she glided to the door and drew a soft breath.

She had expected Luke to appear ill at ease in a suit, but he didn't. He wore a charcoal gray three-piece suit as if he'd been born to it, stepping into her living room with a casual elegance she hadn't anticipated. A snowy white collar glowed against his bronzed skin and below it, an expensive maroon and gray tie. He looked like the president of a huge, sprawling conglomerate. Sam smiled ironically. Why shouldn't he look like a polished successful businessman? After all, he *was* the president of a thriving company.

Luke held her at arm's length and emitted a low admiring whistle. "You are absolutely gorgeous! Turn around and let me see all of you."

Blushing with pleasure, Sam spun lightly between his hands.

"Beautiful!" he breathed. "Absolutely beautiful! You have the longest, most gorgeous legs I've ever seen in my life. Are they new? I don't remember you having legs like that in the mountains."

Laughing, Sam fixed them both a drink, then sat across from him on the sofa. "Same old legs, Bannister. Long enough to reach the floor, just like everybody else's."

"You're not like everybody else, darlin', you're very, very special."

Their eyes met and held, and Sam felt her heart accelerate. She swallowed and ducked her head. "Well? Are you going to tell me what the insurance agent said?" Instantly she regretted the question. She'd promised herself not to mention this issue unless Luke did; she didn't want anything to mar their evening together. But now that she'd blundered into it, she suddenly understood that a great deal depended on his answer.

Luke crossed his ankles and looked at her with an expression she couldn't read. "There's good news and bad news, darlin'. Which do you want first?"

Sam's heart sank. "The bad news first," she said in a low voice. Hopefully the good news would be good enough to compensate.

He swallowed deeply from his glass. "I didn't pay the premium."

"Oh, Luke." In her heart, Sam had guessed as much. But she had desperately wanted to be wrong. She lifted a hand to her lips and stared at him, wondering how his business could sustain such a devastating loss. She didn't know how he could be so calm. In his place, she would have been tearing her hair out and storming around the room like a caged animal.

"But my banker did. That's the good news." Luke's wide mouth curved in an expression of profound relief. "Jim Dobson closed the sale for me while I was on a run to Cheyenne. Jim's a good friend. He assumed I'd want insurance, and further assumed that I hadn't taken care of it. He used the power of attorney I'd given him for the sale to secure insurance."

Sam stared, then the breath rushed from her body. "Thank God!" Her fingers shook as she placed her empty glass on the coffee table. "Thank God." Her dark eyes clouded with something close to accusation. "Do you realize how damned lucky you are? How close you came to disaster?"

"Too close." He rubbed his forehead and she saw how worried he'd been. "I walked into that meeting believing I'd emerge a poorer but wiser man. Believe me, I don't ever want to go through this again."

She heard the sincerity in his tone, saw the conviction in his sobered eyes. And she didn't accept it for a moment. Luke Bannister was a man who would always look to the skies; he wouldn't see the paperwork on his desk. The next time a premium notice appeared, he'd swear to pay it first thing. Then he'd step into a cockpit and forget all life's mundane requirements. And maybe there wouldn't be a good friend on the scene to save him next time. Sam knew this as surely as she knew that no one in the world had eyes as blue as Luke Bannister's.

"I'm happy for you, Luke." Relief drained the tension from between her shoulders. But a look of sadness lingered in her dark eyes. She had wanted so badly to learn that he'd handled his obligations. Himself.

Drawing a deep breath, Sam forced herself to her feet and mustered a smile. After what she and Luke had been through together, they deserved one perfect evening. She made a silent vow not to spoil their dinner by dwelling on thoughts best tucked away for another time.

Luke helped her into her coat, his large, warm hands clasping her shoulders before he released her. Outside, he opened the door of his rental car and smiled at a flash of long legs as Sam slid onto the seat.

"It feels like snow. When we come home, I'll build you a fire." Luke slipped behind the wheel and turned the key.

When we come home . . . Sam stared straight ahead and tried to maintain her smile. Luke laid claim to her home as casually as he'd laid claim to Adams Air. The idea startled her. Since she couldn't imagine Luke at Adams Air, she tried to picture him sharing her townhouse, tried to visualize waiting for him at night, waking to his tousled dark head on the pillow beside her. A delicious shiver rippled up her bared back. And then reality. She suspected their personal habits would mesh no better than their professional habits. Luke probably left the cap off the toothpaste tube, something Sam never did. And she couldn't imagine him making a bed or straightening the kitchen before he left for work.

Annoyed, Sam gave herself a tiny shake. Why was she keying on the negatives tonight? Why was she deliberately opening a distance between them?

Because otherwise she knew she would give in to the strong physical chemistry that made her aware of his smallest motion. And if she did, if she surrendered to the signals her body was receiving, then she was lost, hopelessly lost. She wouldn't be able to remember that their differences were serious and irreconcilable; she would forget that Luke's motives still weren't clear in her mind.

"Sam?" Luke squeezed her cold hand. "Penny for your thoughts?"

"I—I was just wondering if you liked my father." She also wondered what he had thought about Adams Air. Had he inspected her planes and her office and pictured them as his own?

Luke smiled. "I like Frank a lot. Seems we both love the same woman." The pressure on her hand increased. "He's a fine man, Sam. And he knows airplanes like nobody else I've ever met."

"I could tell that he liked you. And Frank Adams is a hard man to please."

Luke's thick eyebrows soared. "I didn't have that impression at all. Your father struck me as easygoing and good-natured."

Sam burst into laughter. "Are we talking about the same person?" She recalled how hard she'd worked this past year trying to please her father and the sense of discouragement at knowing she'd proven a disappointment. The smile faded from her lips.

After braking before the doors to the Chateau Pyrenees, Luke took both her hands in his. "Darlin'," he said softly, looking at her quizzically. "I think there's a problem in communication here. If you really think Frank Adams is hard to please, you should discuss it with him. He's delighted with everything you do."

Now Luke was advising her on family relationships! Sam recoiled, staring hard into his concerned gaze. Luke Bannister was steamrolling her, pushing into all areas of her life. And she didn't know if she was ready for that or even if she wanted it. "It sounds as if you know my father better than I do," she said sharply as she stepped from the car.

Luke relinquished the keys to the parking attendant, then caught her arm. "If I spoke out of turn,

I apologize. Of course I don't know your father better than you do, Sam. I only meant to suggest that maybe this time it's you examining the forest instead of the trees."

"I doubt it," she snapped. She pressed her lips into a tight line, then sighed. Luke thought he was helping, that was all. He couldn't be aware of what she had realized after seeing him with her father—Luke Bannister was the son Frank should have had. The realization had stunned her. She'd experienced an unworthy jealousy that made her feel small and petty, an emotion that had only added to her sense of confusion.

Silently, Sam followed the pressure of Luke's warm hand, climbing the stairs and stepping inside. He checked her coat then they followed the maître d' to a secluded table tucked in an alcove on the upper level. A flurry of waiters appeared, flicking linen napkins across their laps, flourishing menus, and presenting Sam with a long-stemmed red rose. Drinks appeared in a flash.

Remembering her promise to make this a perfect evening, Sam forced herself to relax. Smiling, she raised her eyes from the snowy table and looked out over a small sea of winking candles, startled to discover that she and Luke were the object of covert stares.

"I think we're famous," Luke said, smiling.

The sweetness of a Chopin prelude faded from the piano on the far side of the large room, then the tuxedo-clad pianist moved smoothly into a rendition of "The High and the Mighty."

It appeared to Sam as if every eye in the restaurant swung toward them. She arranged a polite smile on her lips, then nodded at the smattering of applause following the song. She didn't entirely relax again until the pianist returned to his usual program and the diners returned to each other. There was nothing like conducting a romance in a fishbowl, she thought wryly.

To her surprise, Luke was humming softly under his breath as he examined the menu, following the music.

"A man who appreciates both Willie Nelson and Rachmaninoff?" Her lips curved in a genuine smile and she shook her head. "Bannister, you never cease to astonish me."

"That's my plan. I keep you off balance until you fall at my feet."

Sam laughed. "I think your plan is working." He looked impossibly handsome, like Clark Gable posing for a clothing ad. Sam had difficulty recalling how he'd looked in jeans and a sweater.

"Would a beef wellington astonish you? Preceded by escargots and followed by crepes suzette?"

She pretended profound surprise. "What? Naturally, I supposed we'd be dining on those all-time favorites of yours, insects and sour berries."

"That's precisely what I requested when I phoned, but the maître d' informed me the Chateau is fresh out of insects. Escargots were the nearest thing he could offer."

Sam tossed her head and sniffed. "Unforgivable. I hope you told him that henceforth we shall take our business elsewhere."

"I did and the poor man was inconsolable. Unless we promise to return, he is threatening to close the place down."

Smiling at their foolishness, they touched glasses in an unspoken toast. Luke gazed deeply into her sparkling brown eyes then covered her fingers with his large hand. Suddenly Sam's world was right again and the night was spread with magic. Romantic music drifted around them, the food was exqui-

site, and Luke's charm overpowered her earlier
doubts as if nothing had ever occupied her mind but
loving him.

Sam smiled happily over an after-dinner brandy,
wondering where the hours had fled.

"Let's see," Luke said, his eyes capturing the candlelight, "we've toasted the insurance settlement
and having survived the wilds and being rescued
and October and white dresses and gray suits. We've
toasted everything but the most important item.
Us."

"To us," Sam murmured. She sipped her brandy
and smiled radiantly. His admiring gaze made her
feel beautiful and cherished.

"The moment has come, darlin', to solidify our
future."

A tiny cloud of uneasiness stole across Sam's
pleasure. "I think I'd like a dozen more evenings as
perfect as this one before we make any definite
plans," Sam said, keeping her tone light. "There's no
need to rush things, is there?"

"I know what I want, Sam, and it isn't going to
change after a dozen dinners or two dozen or a thousand. I love you. The thing I want most in this world
is to marry you."

"There's no hurry, is there?" Sam asked in a small
voice. She still wasn't comfortable with the idea of
love at first sight. And the thought of relinquishing
control at Adams Air sent a chill down her spine.
The bottom line was she didn't think she could do it.
She couldn't give away Adams Air, not to any man.
Not after she'd invested so much work, so many
dreams.

Luke smiled, his face lighting with love. "Take
your time, darlin', and plan whatever kind of
wedding you want. You just tell me where to show up
and when and I'll be there."

"Luke, we've got to talk about . . ."

Smiling broadly, Luke nodded to the waiter standing behind Sam's chair. With a flourish, the waiter bowed and presented Sam a crystal tray covered by a silver dome.

"What's this?" Sam frowned at the waiter. "I didn't order dessert."

"I ordered something for you," Luke said softly. "I hope you'll like it."

Sam raised an inquiring eyebrow, then she lifted the silver dome. A small box rested within. With shaking hands, Sam eased open the lid then smothered a gasp. A magnificent diamond solitaire sparkled against a blue velvet lining.

"Oh, Luke," she breathed softly.

"If you don't like the setting, we can exchange it," he said anxiously. "Or if it isn't the right size."

"No, no. It's lovely. Beautiful." Slowly she removed the ring and slipped it onto her finger. It fit perfectly. Luke smiled as she turned her hand, watching the candlelight flash from the stone. "Luke, I—I don't know what to say."

"Say you'll marry me," he laughed. "Say that you'll slap any man silly who dares to look at you. Say you love me."

Her eyes softened. "Oh, Luke, Luke. I do love you. No matter what happens, I do love you."

"What will happen is that we're going to be married, have two point three children, and live happily ever after." He gazed at her, love shining from his vibrant blue eyes. Sam's breath caught in her throat. "Let's go home, darlin'," he said in a husky voice.

She nodded helplessly.

Outside, a black sky was spitting small, hard flakes of snow. The air was cold and damp against Sam's flushed cheeks.

"Perfect!" Luke exclaimed, handing her into the car. "The night of the first snow is always magic."

When they'd returned to Sam's townhouse, he knelt before the fireplace. "I'll build us a fire while you find that bottle of brandy you promised." He blew Sam a kiss, then removed his jacket and loosened his tie.

Moving in a daze, acutely conscious of the ring on her finger, Sam loaded the stereo with soft music, then turned out the lights and opened the patio draperies. She couldn't quite believe it; she was engaged. She tried to recall her earlier doubts, but when Luke was near her, she seemed incapable of thinking of anything but him. Blinking, she watched the blowing snow hiss lightly against the patio panes. A blazing fire crackled behind her, spreading a romantic glow throughout the room.

She started as Luke's hands slipped around her waist and he gently pulled her into the hard curve of his body. They stood together watching the snow, then his lips brushed her hair and his large hands slid upward to cup her breasts. "I've been wanting to do this all night," he murmured.

Sam's dark lashes squeezed against her cheekbones as a wave of dizziness swept her body. If only it could always be like this, she thought frantically. If only it could be this simple and uncomplicated, this direct and basic. Turning in his arms, she raised parted lips and met his kiss with an eagerness that hinted at desperation. She moaned softly as his hands slipped up her bare back, then trailed teasingly along her spine.

"Sam, my beautiful Sam," he whispered hoarsely. Slowly his hands slid the white jersey from her shoulders and the material slithered to her waist, exposing her breasts to the peach glow of firelight. He sucked in his breath and groaned softly. His fingers shook slightly as he fumbled with her belt. In a moment her dress dropped to a soft puddle at her feet, and she stood in her garters and nylons before him, her trembling fingers pulling at his tie.

When Luke was as naked as she, Sam looked at him, loving the long, clean lines of his body, his strength and grace. She stepped into his arms, the action as natural and right as breathing, and she felt the heat of the fire on his firm skin and the heat of passion on his lips. A low cry broke from her throat as he gently lifted her in his arms, then laid her on the rug before the fire, rocking back on his heels to look at her.

"You're so lovely," he whispered, his voice ragged with desire. "So utterly lovely."

Sam lifted her arms to him and her eager body arched of its own accord. She wanted him with an urgency that was almost painful. "Please, Luke . . ."

He stretched out beside her, his black hair shining in the fire glow, and he pressed her along the hard length of his body, tasting her skin with tiny flicks of his tongue.

"Luke, Luke . . ." Sam whispered his name without being aware that she spoke as his lips roamed slowly over her aching body, tantalizing, teasing. His darting tongue coaxed her nipples into hard, rosy peaks, then descended lower until she felt the brush of his lips across her inner thighs, igniting fires deep within. She bit her lips to keep from crying out as his mouth covered her center and teased her to heights she'd never before imagined climbing. And when she thought surely her mind and body would explode, he allowed her the release she begged for and then gathered her shuddering body into his arms and stroked her until she quieted.

When she could breathe normally, Sam turned her attention to teasing Luke as he had teased her. She began at his eyelids, covering his face with lingering kisses, then she nibbled light kisses over his throat and chest. When her searching mouth slipped below his navel, Luke groaned and raised his head, staring down at her dark curls. "Sam," he whispered. "Are you sure? You don't have to . . ."

But she wanted to. For the first time in her life she wanted to give pleasure as completely as she had received. Gently she took him into her mouth until his hands reached to pull her up on top of him.

"Oh God, Sam. I love you so much!"

He entered her quickly, urgently, and their bodies sought familiar rhythms, matching pace and need. Sam hadn't believed their lovemaking could be better than it had been, but tonight it was a symphony. They played familiar instruments, creating a blissful harmony she hadn't dreamed possible. And when the crescendo swelled, she cried his name and her fingers dug into his shoulders and she teetered on the rim of a splendid joy so intense she thought she could not bear it and survive.

"You and I just get better and better," Luke murmured when they had showered and wrapped themselves in fluffy bath sheets. He relaxed against the sofa and smiled at the firelight illuminating her shining face.

"Hmmm," Sam agreed drowsily, watching the fire dance in the grate. She curled deeper into his arms and nestled her head on his shoulder, listening to the whisper of snow striking the window panes, to the comfortable snap of popping logs. She wished time would stop, wished the night would never end.

"Will you come to Aspen next weekend?"

Sam nodded. Her fingers curled in the hair covering his chest, and she inhaled the soapy smell of his skin. A stirring of desire quickened her breath. And she laughed softly as the towel slipped across his lap and she saw his own awakening.

"You're insatiable," she smiled as he growled softly, then swept her into his arms and stood.

"With you I am." He held her as easily as if she were a child. "Where is your bedroom, darlin'? Do you realize we haven't yet made love in an honest-to-God bed like normal people?"

Sam laughed against his naked shoulder and pointed. "I think we're duty bound to give it a try."

Luke was gone when she awoke. For a moment Sam experienced a sense of disorientation, then she remembered he'd booked an early flight. She stretched, taking pleasure in the unaccustomed sensuality of her naked skin against the printed sheets. Then she tied a robe about her waist and padded toward the kitchen to start the coffee before she showered.

She halted abruptly at the door to the living room. Crumpled towels covered her sofa, the sticky brandy glasses were still on the coffee table. Her white dress hung limply across a chair back, her nylons and shoes lay in a tangle before the fireplace.

Sinking to a counter stool, Sam stared at the mess in dismay. What kind of enchantment did Luke Bannister induce to make her abandon the habits of a lifetime? She'd never gone to bed without straightening her living room. She hated waking to a mess. Chewing her lip, Sam slowly proceeded into the kitchen and plugged in the coffeepot. Then she rinsed the brandy glasses and placed them in the dishwasher.

After gathering her clothing, she returned to her bedroom. And she made a wager with herself that Luke had left the cap off the toothpaste.

He had. He had also left a note taped to her bathroom mirror: "Good morning, darlin'. Seeing you sleeping next to me made this a morning to treasure. A lifetime of waking to you won't be enough. I love you, Sam. I'm counting the hours until the weekend. Luke."

She studied his broad, bold scrawl, then closed her eyes and released a long breath. Luke Bannister was an enigma. He thought to leave her a love note, but apparently he hadn't noticed the dirty glasses in the living room. He took the trouble to arrange the presentation of the ring, but couldn't remember to arrange insurance. He stole her clients then told her how to beat him at his own game.

How could she understand such a man? How could she ever hope to live with him?

Sighing, Sam replaced the cap on the toothpaste tube then stared hard at the ring flashing on her finger.

"Oh, Luke," she whispered, feeling a sting of tears behind her eyes. "I don't know, I just don't know . . ."

She'd never felt so confused in her life.

They were so utterly different. Too different. Sam leaned against the counter top and dropped her head. They would drive each other crazy—and the craziness would destroy everything that was good and right. Eventually they had to face the fact that they agreed on few items. Business was a bone of contention; so were personal habits. Sooner or later, the points of divergence would assume a destructive importance.

She lifted her head and stared into the mirror, watching tears brim into her eyes.

It simply wasn't going to work.

The pain of loving him washed over her in sharp, slicing waves. But Sam knew there was more to life than loving. There was work. And insurance. And dirty glasses in the morning.

She covered her face and wept.

Chapter Thirteen

Sam twisted the ring on her finger and listened to the drone of the airplane's engines. Dropping her head to the back of the seat, she closed her lashes, dreading the upcoming confrontation with Luke.

After agonizing through every minute of the past week, vacillating wildly from one hour to the next, Sam had finally, painfully, concluded that she couldn't marry Luke Bannister.

Luke had phoned every night, and every night Sam had tried to tell him what she'd decided. Each time she had faltered. And after each call, she had paced about her bedroom wishing she had never accepted his ring; it had been a mistake. She'd known from the beginning they weren't right for each other. Emotion had clouded her judgment.

Finally, she'd concluded that telling him on the phone was the coward's way out. She had to tell him in person; she owed him that much.

Chewing her lower lip, Sam stared at her twisting hands rather than glance from the window at the rocky terrain gliding past below. Memories she resisted invaded her thoughts. She remembered yodeling happily atop the rock and the naked water fight—and tender nights, glorious nights. So many small precious moments. After waging a mental battle, she gave in with a helpless shake of her head and reviewed their relationship from the beginning, as she'd been doing all week.

The same troubling conclusions surfaced with disturbing clarity. Item one: Bannister had claimed her from the beginning—but Sam didn't trust love at first sight. Item two: Bannister's company was smaller than Adams Air; Luke would benefit most from a marriage merger. Item three: she couldn't, absolutely could not, relinquish Adams Air into the hands of a man so careless with crucial business requisites. Item four: she and Luke would drive each other crazy. She would want him to replace the toothpaste cap and he would never understand why it was important.

Sam rolled her head across the seat and gazed out at the wintry blue sky. The most upsetting item constricted her chest and raised a lump to her throat. She loved him.

But she was no longer naive enough to believe love conquered all. Love was a fragile trust in constant danger from outside threats. Her love for Luke Bannister would come under siege whenever business was discussed, whenever her orderly mind clashed with his spontaneity. She would worry herself sick wondering what he was doing with the company she and her father had worked to build. Worst of all, she would always wonder which he had wanted most: Samantha Adams or Adams Air.

Eventually, their love would sour to bitterness and accusation. And that was something she could not bear. It was kinder and more sensible to end their relationship now rather than wait until a wall of acrimony had grown between them, brick by resentful brick, until their emotions and their businesses were hopelessly tangled.

Heart aching, Sam stepped from the plane and steeled herself against the leap of emotion drawing her breath when she saw Luke standing at the foot of the ramp. His eyes lit when he saw her, and Sam's

heart sank even as her body responded with a traitorous sensual tingle.

"Sam, darlin'." He clasped her into his wide,
strong arms and held her tightly. "God, I've missed
you!"

And then his warm, hungry lips were covering
hers and Sam felt the strength rushing from her
body. Her resolve wavered and she met his kiss with
a desperate eagerness that dismayed her.

When Luke released her, she looked up at him
with a shaky smile, seeing the winter sun in his
black hair, the confident, strong smile curving his
lips. The time wasn't right, she told herself frantically. She couldn't step off the plane and hand him his
ring with no explanation. And she couldn't hope to
explain anything while her body trembled with fire
and yearning.

"We'll collect your luggage, then I'll show you my
office." He tucked her arm around his and covered
her fingers with his hand. "I'm saving my condo for
last."

Sam didn't dare go home with him. If she did, she
knew she wouldn't be able to tell him what she had
decided. Her physical need for him would get in the
way. And delaying would only intensify the ache in
her heart. "I didn't bring any luggage," she said in a
low voice.

Luke misunderstood. His mouth curved in a wide
delighted grin and he slid his arm around her waist
and hugged her close. "All you need is a toothbrush."
His eyes slid over her, lingering for a moment on the
long sweep of her legs. "You're even more beautiful
than I remembered," he said in a gruff whisper.
"How did I get so lucky?"

Every word he spoke drove a dagger into Sam's
heart. She wished he wouldn't look at her like she
was a treasure, wished he wasn't so obviously

delighted to see her. Most of all, she wished she didn't feel so damned guilty. Biting her lip hard, she followed Luke to the cart beside the terminal and climbed onto the seat beside him, only half listening to what he said.

Her eyes scanned the snow-dusted mountains as he drove toward the freight offices and she absently agreed they'd been fortunate not to have crashed after the snow fell. Inwardly, she castigated herself for feeling guilty. Her decision had not been easy or hasty. She had agonized for long, thoughtful hours. Ending it would be best for them both; she believed this utterly. So why did it hurt so much? Why did she dread telling him?

Nervously, Sam touched her purse, reassuring herself that her return ticket was safely within. She had four hours before her flight returned to Denver. Four hours in which to muster her courage and do the right thing.

They climbed from the cart before a long, low building at the edge of the field and crunched over a light crust of snow toward a row of doors beneath painted signs. One announced Bannister Air Freight.

"This is it," Luke said grandly, pushing open the door. "The home office of Bannister Air, that small but promising company of the future."

Sam stepped into a one-room office smaller than Marva's cubicle. Her own office was three times the size. She made a small sound in the back of her throat and gazed around her.

Maps covered the walls, most of them with colored tacks pinned above city names, others strictly topographical. A ragged sign-in sheet hung from a clipboard by the door, scrawled over with pilots' names, times, routes. Files were stacked everywhere, even on the floor. The disorder stunned Sam.

The side chairs were amost hidden by books and maps; Bannister's desk was simply a disaster.

Papers spilled everywhere without any apparent attempt at organization. Unlike her own desk, Luke's had no baskets to separate memos, invoices, bills of lading, flight charts, and so on.

Appalled, Sam raised a pale face. "Bannister, this is—this is awful! How do you find anything? How do you know what you're hauling, or where it's going and when?" Her hands lifted, then fell. "How in the world do you keep track of your accounts? Or even find your ledger?"

Luke clasped his chest with both hands and grinned down at her. "A stab to the heart. And after I worked all morning to clean this up for you."

Sam shook her head, her eyes wide and frowning. "You need a secretary. And more space."

He nodded cheerfully. "I suppose I could evict Michelson next door and take over his office, but he's a good tenant and . . ."

Sam stared. "You *own* this building?"

Luke smiled. "I wasn't always a freight magnate, my love. For a while I was a real estate tycoon." He shrugged modestly. "I own a real estate company in town. Lois Ames runs it; a sharp lady. Once in a while something comes along that Lois thinks I should buy . . ."

"You own a real estate company?" Sam repeated. Bannister continued to surprise her. She pushed a hand through her hair and blinked.

"And a chocolate shop."

"A chocolate shop?"

"I like chocolate." Bannister took her arm and flicked off the lights. "In fact, I'll take you there. Kate Byers makes the best chocolates you ever tasted."

Sam glanced at his desk, itching to sit down and

straighten out the mess. She didn't know how anyone could run a business in the midst of such chaos. Slowly, she followed Luke out the door and toward the parking lot.

"How do you find time for chocolate and real estate and hauling freight?"

"I don't. I hire good people to do it for me." He opened the jeep door and handed her inside.

Sam bit her lip and stared at the windshield, remembering that he'd said he couldn't wait until she cleaned up his office. Was she just another of the "good people" he positioned to care for his interests?

She turned troubled eyes to his profile. "Why haven't you hired a good secretary?"

After wheeling the jeep onto the highway, Luke smiled at her. "When I'm busy enough to need a secretary, I don't have time to find one. And, as you pointed out, I really don't have space for another desk. I've got to do something about that."

Same gave herself a shake. It didn't matter. After today, she reminded herself, Luke Bannister would not be her concern. The thought twisted like a knife through her heart. "Why didn't you mention the chocolate shop and the real estate before?"

"I thought I had." He looked at her in surprise. "I didn't? Shows you where my heart is," he laughed. "Up there."

Sam stared at him in astonishment. When Luke Bannister thought about flying everything else vanished from his mind. A sense of depression settled over her shoulders. The sooner she returned his ring, the better. Seeing his office had only confirmed her conviction that they could never make it together. She stared ahead through aching eyes as he spun the jeep into a space before a remodeled Victorian building that looked as if it were made of gingerbread.

The Chocolate Rabbit was warm and cheerful

inside and smelled of half-forgotten childhood dreams. The fragrance of fudge and taffy and cinnamon cookies spiced each breath. Sparkling glass counters displayed platters of every conceivable chocolate confection. Colorful jars of jelly beans and taffy and penny-candy stretched along the back shelves above glass-topped bins of homemade cookies.

"See why I like it here?" Luke smiled.

Sam nodded and seated herself near a window. Pale sunlight fell across the small table and stroked the green plants hanging from the ceiling. When Luke returned from the counter, Sam looked at him and her chest constricted with a bittersweet ache. He held a peanut-butter cookie in one large hand and a steaming cup of hot chocolate in the other. He was smiling happily.

Dear God. How could she do this? An expression of sheer misery drained the color from her face. Then quickly, before she could change her mind, Sam twisted the ring from her finger and placed it on the table between them.

"I can't marry you, Luke," she blurted, her voice as thin and drawn as her expression.

Luke's smile faded as he realized she was serious. Slowly he lowered the cookie to his plate and pushed aside his cup. "What's wrong, darlin'? What's this all about?"

Fighting to maintain a level tone, Sam listed the items she'd rehearsed on the plane. And she prayed he would understand and recognize the truth of what she was saying. What she hadn't rehearsed was the pain, the sharp agonizing slash across her heart.

Luke listened silently until she had finished. "There's nothing you've mentioned that we can't work out." He reached to cover her shaking fingers with his large, square hand. "As long as we love each other. Do you love me, Sam?"

She drew a long, miserable breath. "There's one more thing." The diamond ring flashed in the sunlight, lying between them like an accusation. "I . . ."

"Go ahead, say it."

Sam wet her lips then looked into his eyes. "I'm not completely sure if it's me you want—or my business."

They stared at each other across the small table and Sam felt her nerves grow taut. She wished to heaven that she knew what he was thinking. His large hands had curled into fists beside his cookie and hot chocolate. His blue eyes had turned strangely flat and shuttered.

"Let me understand this," Luke said slowly. "You think I'm a fraud? That everything I've said or done from the beginning was a lie? Calculated for the sole purpose of stealing Adams Air?"

Sam's jaw tightened. Her own hands formed fists in her lap. "People don't fall in love at first sight . . . I just don't know." She bit her lip and looked at him unhappily. "I know we don't mesh, Luke. We don't think alike, and . . ."

"Wait a minute. I need to know if you really think I'm the kind of man who would marry a woman to further his own ambitions."

"I—I don't know." Sam's voice had sunk to a whisper.

"You don't know?"

She heard the disbelief in his voice, and then the hurt. And she knew her worst fears were becoming reality. She had hoped to end as friends, with dignity—but it wasn't going to happen.

Sam pushed at her hair and looked away from the anger growing in Luke's gaze. It seemed incredible to her that business proceeded as usual in the chocolate shop, that children danced in the door and handed up a dollar in exchange for a plump bag of jelly beans and chocolate creams, that the girl behind the counter continued to smile and laugh. Sunshine flooded through the windows and the shop smelled warm and wonderful. And it all struck Sam as ludicrous. Her world was crumbling in the middle of a candy shop.

Luke stared at her for what seemed an eternity, searching her eyes for assurances she couldn't give. Then he reached for the ring and his fingers closed around it.

Pride stiffened his shoulders and cooled his gaze. With something near panic, Sam watched the blue of a summer day chill to the icy hue of a winter pond; his expression was angry and distant.

"You should know I'm not that kind of man, Sam. That you could even ask the question hurts. It hurts deeply."

Sam's hands fluttered up from her lap. "You can see why I don't think we should . . ."

"You're damned right I can see." He pushed his fingers into his pocket and when his hand reappeared, the ring was gone. "It never occurred to me that you thought I was after your business. Not once did I suppose you thought I was that dishonest and insensitive."

"Luke . . ."

"Let me tell you something, Sam. I'm going to build the biggest and the best air freight company in the Rocky Mountain region with or without you and Adams Air. And I'll do it honorably and honestly."

"I didn't mean to imply . . ."

"Sure you did." Anger blazed like icy fire in his eyes. "Combining our businesses might have helped both of us to reach our goals a little sooner, that's all it meant to me. I believed we could combine our skills. I never intended to wrest your precious company away from you."

Sam swallowed hard. "Luke, I don't think . . ."

"You think I was hustling you from the first. You've made that damned clear."

Sam stared into the condemnation hardening his expression and felt a burst of anger. Her jaw tightened defensively. "You have to admit you came on pretty strong that first day. Declaring you were going to marry me practically before I'd said a word. What did you suppose I would think?"

"I'd hoped you'd be flattered. I'd hoped you'd recognize the truth when you heard it. But I've been fighting you from the beginning. If you don't trust me and never have, then why in the hell did you say you loved me?" His cool gaze flicked over her pale face as he leaned backward in his chair.

"Oh, Luke," There was no point in continuing. Sam closed her lashes for a brief moment, fighting the urge to turn and run.

"Now I understand why you seemed to fear a commitment. You were protecting Adams Air from the greedy bastard who wanted to take it away from you." He stared at her. "Isn't that a little arrogant, Sam? Adam Air isn't exactly a household word—if I was willing to fake a romance to build my business in a hurry, I'd do better to marry the daughter of whoever owns Emery, wouldn't I?"

"*I'm* arrogant?" Sam's dark eyes flashed. She leaned her elbows on the table and hunched over them. "How about you, Bannister? You announce you're going to marry me, and I'm supposed to fall into a swoon of gratitude. You told me you'd put me out of business if I didn't marry you—isn't that just a little arrogant? And how about all that talk about how I'm supposed to step in and rescue your office? And your assumptions about my home and Adams

Air?" She paused for breath. "Of course I've been fighting you. You're like a steamroller ignoring everything in your path. You've never asked what I want!"

Tight lines bracketed his mouth. "I assumed that you wanted the same thing I did. Or did I imagine that you said you loved me?"

Sam shoved a hand through her hair and lowered her voice. She hated what was happening between them, absolutely hated it. "I do love you. I just—I—"

"In some circles love means trust," he said levelly.

Frustration raised a lump to her throat. "How can I trust that you would operate Adams Air any more efficiently than you run your own business?" A tightness banded Sam's chest. She saw the anger in his eyes, felt his hostility lashing out at her. "Luke, my father devoted his life to Adams Air, and I've worked hard too. And . . ."

He lifted a hand. "I get the picture, Sam. Luke Bannister would ruin everything you and Frank have worked to achieve."

She stared at him, angry that he was making this so difficult. "Of course I'm worried! I'm worried you'll forget the insurance on one of my planes, worried that my office will end by looking like yours!"

Knots ran up his jawline. "When you—no, make that *if* you ever pictured us married, where did you see yourself?" His voice remained low but sharp. He leaned toward her over the table. "In case it matters, I saw you handling office administration and me handling flight operations. I saw us working together, utilizing our particular talents. I've never seen you as a retired housewife sitting quietly on the sidelines."

The issue had never been resolved in Sam's mind. Sometimes she had visualized herself trying to work with Luke, other times she had pictured herself pushed out of the business. She opened her lips to speak, then halted at the expression on Luke's face.

"Let's end this, Sam. We can sit here and hurl accusations until we're both bleeding inside, but I don't think either of us wants to do that." He passed a hand over his eyes and when his fingers dropped, his face was weary. Defeated. The expression lasted an instant, then was replaced by a firm-jawed pride. "I'm not going to beg anyone to be my wife. I accept your decision." He shrugged, striving for a nonchalant attitude.

"I just don't think we could make a go of it. We'll end by . . ."

"I think you've made your point, Sam."

"Oh Luke, I didn't want this to be ugly." And she hadn't dreamed the pain would be so intense. That she saw the same pain mirrored in Luke's eyes only made it worse. She felt as if an iron vise had closed around her breast, cutting off her breath, squeezing her heart.

"It's not easy hearing that you think I'm just using you." The bitterness in his voice caused Sam to wince. Luke clenched his jaw and stared at the ceiling, obviously striving for control. "Look, Sam, I'm sorry." Abruptly, he pushed back his chair and stood. "I'll take you out to the airport. I assume you're going home immediately?"

"Yes," Sam whispered. "But I can catch a cab."

"Is that what you want?"

"I . . ." Oh God, she didn't know what she wanted. Everything had seemed so clear-cut and obvious, and now nothing seemed clear. She felt as if the ground had fallen away beneath her.

Stumbling to her feet, Sam followed him and silently climbed into the jeep. Without speaking, they drove to Sardy Field and Luke waited while she checked in for her flight. He walked outside with her and they stood beside the ramp as the other passengers boarded.

"I'm sorry, Luke. It just won't work." Sam looked up into his hard face and told herself that she absolutely would not cry. She would not give in to the tears stinging her eyelids and thickening her voice. "We'd drive each other crazy, we'd . . ."

He placed a finger across her lips, stopping the flow of explanations. The back of his hand gently stroked her cheek then his arm fell to his side. "Good-bye, Sam."

She stared into his eyes and knew they had said all there was to say. It was over. She looked at him and wanted to fling her arms around his neck and hold on forever. Instead she turned woodenly and walked up the stairs, feeling his eyes on her back.

He was still standing at the foot of the ramp when she settled herself into her seat and leaned to the window. For a long moment their eyes held, then Luke gave her a jaunty salute and turned away. He thrust his hands deep into his pockets and walked toward the freight buildings, his head down, his boots kicking at the snow.

Sam watched until the engines whined to life and the plane rolled toward the runway. Then she stared at nothing, her fingers clamped over the edges of the armrests. And she saw him holding the cookie, then watched again as his fingers closed over the ring. The awful finality of his good-bye echoed in her ear.

She covered her face with her hands and wept.

Chapter Fourteen

❧

Marva placed a letter on Sam's desk and pushed her arms into her coat sleeves. "If you'll sign that I'll drop it in the box on my way out."

Sam glanced up in surprise. "You're leaving now?" She couldn't remember when Marva had last left exactly at five. "Are you and Bill going out to dinner?"

Marva didn't look at her. "No. It's just been a long day."

Sam nodded agreement. All the days had seemed long recently. And the nights, the endless nights. Frowning, Sam signed the letter then looked up at Marva. "I've been a bear, haven't I?" She leaned back in her chair and sighed. To say she'd been irritable and jumpy lately was to understate the case. "I'm sorry, Marva. I've just—I've had a lot on my mind."

Marva tilted her head and studied the delicate shadows beneath Sam's eyes. "You know, boss," she said lightly. "It wouldn't hurt you to go home at a decent hour yourself. When Bill and I drove by here on the way home from the movies last night, your office light was still burning."

Sam had worked late every night for two weeks, hoping work would keep her mind off Luke Bannister. And sometimes she was successful. Occasionally she glanced at the clock and congratulated herself that she hadn't thought about him for hours. But eventually she had to go home to her meticulously tidy townhouse with its silent telephone, and its big, lonely bed.

"Marva, please sit with me a minute." Sam was appalled by the obvious plea of loneliness in her tone. Rubbing at the fatigue smudging her eyes, she waited gratefully as Marva obligingly removed her coat and poured them both a cup of coffee.

Marva lit a cigarette in the silence, then drew a long breath. "Well. Am I mistaken or did we sign three new accounts this week?" When Sam continued to stare into her cup without speaking, Marva commented gently, "Sometimes it helps to talk . . ."

"Does Bill screw the cap back on the toothpaste?" The question astounded Sam as much as Marva. She could have kicked herself.

"Lord, no," Marva laughed. "And he's never put a dish in the dishwasher or picked up his shoes either. What man does?"

"Some do," Sam said slowly. Biting her lip, she examined Marva's cheerful smile. "Doesn't it drive you crazy?"

"Sure. I have days when I'd like to pick up a skillet and pound him into the carpet."

Sam nodded miserably.

"But then I think about all the times Bill cooks dinner when he thinks I'm tired." Marva's wise eyes examined Sam's face. "And all the roses he's sent over the years—enough to fill a greenhouse. And what a wonderful father he was when the kids were home." She shrugged. "And then I think maybe it isn't too important that he never remembers to rinse out the coffeepot." She paused a moment, then added softly, "A lot of women would give anything to come home to a kiss and a hug, even if it meant picking up shoes and dirty glasses."

Sam stared. "No one's perfect, right?"

"No one is."

"But what if Bill overlooked paying the mortgage? What if he never posted accounts or—or kept track of important items?"

"Then I guess I'd pay the mortgage and post the accounts." Marva read the resistance in Sam's frown. "Honey, marriage isn't a fifty-fifty proposition. Whoever said that is full of baloney. Both partners have to be willing to do whatever it takes without keeping score. I do what I'm good at, and Bill does what he's good at. Is it a fair division? I don't know. I don't really think it matters."

Sam bit her lower lip and tapped a pencil against the desktop. "Love conquers all," she said, hating the sarcasm in her voice.

"No, love is the reward for recognizing what's important and what isn't." After stubbing out her cigarette, Marva stood and reached for her coat. "Would Bill be a better man if he replaced the toothpaste cap? Would rinsing out the coffeepot make him kinder or more lovable? Somehow I don't think so." She buttoned her coat. "I think I'll keep him just as he is."

After Marva departed, Sam poured another coffee and leaned back in her chair. All right, how important was a toothpaste cap and all that it symbolized? Which would she rather have—a tidy house or Luke? The question was ridiculous. Even when she thought about insurance premiums, she knew Marva was right: Sam could handle the business details herself. And she could hire a housekeeper.

These small questions were the least of her concerns. Did Luke love her? That was the central issue—did he really love her? If she could only know for certain, if she could only trust in love at first sight. She wished to heaven that she had some guarantee Luke wasn't another Brad Jennings.

Tenting her fingers beneath her chin, Sam stared

at the wall and allowed herself to remember Brad. Ambitious, greedy Brad of the glib tongue and easy promises. She had believed every word, had ignored all the warning signs until even she could no longer pretend Brad wasn't using her. When she'd accused him of wanting Adams Air more than her, Brad had protested vehemently.

Why hadn't Luke protested? Why hadn't he tried to convince her that he wasn't interested in Adams Air?

Because it would have been a lie.

Angrily, Sam pushed from the desk. She was driving herself mad with the same questions, over and over again. And always she reached the same painful conclusion: she'd done the right thing. She and Luke couldn't possibly have made a success of marriage.

Rising, she straightened her desk, then rinsed her coffee mug and slipped into her coat. A glance at the clock told her she would be late for dinner with her parents.

At least she had three new accounts to report. Maybe the news would please her father.

Frank Adams looked decidedly bored. Sam's voice trailed as she concluded her report, and she felt the familiar frustration of discouragement. Without understanding why, she knew she'd let her father down. Again.

"That's nice, honey," Frank commented politely. "You're doing a fine job."

If she was doing such a fine job then why didn't she feel like it? Why didn't her father seem genuinely pleased or even interested?

"We have a chance to bid on Consolidated Bakeries, Dad. It could be our biggest account yet."

Frank waved at a friend standing near the restaurant bar and his face lit. "Will you ladies excuse me for a minute?"

Sam's face clouded in an expression of confusion as she watched her father cross the restaurant. "Damn!"

Natalie Adams sipped her wine and glanced at Sam's hand, tactfully refraining from inquiring about the missing solitaire. "You seem a little on edge tonight, Samantha. Are you sleeping well?"

"Why can't I please him, Mom?" Sam's hands curled into fists, then she rubbed her eyes. "I try, but nothing I do seems to be enough."

Wine spilled over Natalie's fingers and she stared at her daughter in astonishment. "Samantha Adams! What on earth are you talking about? Your father boasts about your success to anyone who will listen—he's very, very proud of what you've accomplished."

Sam pushed a weary hand through her dark hair. "Dad hardly listens to what I tell him. It's as if he doesn't want to know how the business is doing."

"Frankly, dear, he doesn't." Natalie reached to cover her daughter's hand. "But it has nothing to do with you. Your father has *never* cared about accounts or business negotiations."

Sam shook her head. Lifting her knife, she drew aimless patterns on the tablecloth. "I wish I could believe that. But if it was totally true, there wouldn't be an Adams Air Freight company."

Natalie smiled, the candlelight smoothing years from her soft face. "Samantha, may I ask how many accounts you've added in the past year?"

"I don't know. Twenty? Thirty?"

"And how many did you inherit when you took over the business?"

"Maybe a hundred, I never counted them."

Natalie swirled the wine in her glass. "Has it ever

occurred to you to to wonder how you could add thirty accounts in one year when your father only signed a hundred in nearly twenty years?"

The knife dropped from Sam's fingers. She stared at her mother.

"Darling, your father is a wonderful man, but he's a pilot, not a salesman. Adams Air provided us a comfortable living, but it certainly didn't make us rich. I didn't care because your father was happy, doing what he wanted to do." Natalie smiled toward the bar. "Your father and I are very proud that you are building Adams Air into all it can be. Frank always said the potential was there—he just wasn't the right person to develop it."

Sam looked toward the bar also, watching her father throw back his head and laugh. A hundred accounts. Good lord, why hadn't she seen it? Of course he was bored with her reports; all she talked about was this account and that account. She'd been seeking his approval on a subject that put him to sleep. No wonder he didn't respond as she wished him to.

Her father was no more business-oriented than Luke Bannister. She simply had refused to notice. And now that she had, did that make her think any less of Frank Adams? Of course not.

Continuing to work it out in her mind, Sam gazed into Natalie's clear eyes. "Thank you, Mom," she said in a low voice. Sam was not her father's son. She never had been, and he had never wanted her to be. She wasn't like him at all. Something tight splintered and fell away from her heart. She was her own person, successful in her own right. Why on earth hadn't she realized it sooner?

"I've been looking to Dad for approval," she said slowly, scarcely aware that she was speaking aloud. "But the issues aren't important to anyone but me. I don't need Dad's approval, only my own." Amazed, she blinked into her mother's smile. "I've been an idiot."

Natalie laughed. "You could never be an idiot." Now she allowed herself a pointed glance at Sam's fingers. "Unless you let Clark Gable get away. Do you want to talk about him?"

The sharp ache that surfaced whenever Sam thought of Luke lodged in her throat. "Not yet. Thanks for caring, but . . . I can't talk about it just yet." Time would ease the pain of missing him—but it hadn't happened yet.

When Frank returned to the table, Sam regarded him with fresh insight. She thought a moment then smiled. "Dad, did I tell you about Ellis McCarther breaking open the crates of baby chickens when he landed at Boise?"

Frank laughed. "Ellis landed that hard? What was he flying? A tank?"

Sam drew a breath. *"Louise."*

"Louise always did have a heavy touch. She has a tail like a chunk of lead." Smiling with pleasure, he leaned forward eagerly. "Did the chicks get out of the hold?"

As Sam told the story, she watched the sparkle in her father's eyes, felt his laughter like a healing balm. This was what he wanted to hear, what he missed about Adams Air. She been a fool, a blind fool. Like Luke, her father was more interested in flying than he would ever be in even the most exciting new account. Reaching into her memory, Sam pulled up other stories, incidents she'd thought he wouldn't be interested in hearing, and her father listened eagerly.

"Excuse me, sir." The waiter cleared his throat discreetly. "We're about to close, would you like anything more from the bar?"

"Good heavens. It's almost midnight." Sam blinked in surprise. In the past, Frank had ended business evenings early by expressing a desire to hurry home for the ten o'clock news.

Tonight, he looked distinctly disappointed instead of relieved as he paid the tab and they walked to the parking lot. "Honey, this was wonderful. I don't know when I've enjoyed myself more." He hugged her. "Your mother and I are so proud of you."

Tears sprang into Sam's dark eyes. She'd heard the words a thousand times. Why hadn't she believed them before now? When her mother leaned to kiss her cheek, Sam embraced her warmly. "How can I ever thank you?" she whispered.

Natalie brushed a lock of dark hair from her daughter's cheek. "Just be happy."

Just be happy. Her mother's wish echoed in Sam's inner ear throughout the weekend. Being happy had somehow gotten mixed up with Luke Bannister.

Sam cleaned her townhouse in a whirlwind of scrubbing and polishing, hoping to keep her thoughts well away from Bannister. But everything reminded her of him. Annoyed, she slipped the Willie Nelson recordings into their jackets and loaded the stereo with easy listening music that shouldn't have reminded her of anything. But it did: memories of snuggling in oversized towels watching the fire flooded her thoughts.

Sinking onto a stool and pulling a coffee cup across the counter, Sam decided it was hopeless. Everything reminded her of Luke. The snow melting down the patio panes. The fire snapping in the grate. Her carpet. Her sofa. Her bed.

Her big empty bed. Feeling the sting of unshed tears, Sam watched her fingers clench into a fist. She had never realized how lonely it was to lie in the darkness and listen to the silence. Or to touch a vacant pillow.

Restless, she pushed from the counter and wandered to stand before her aquarium. "You guys are lousy pets, you know that? You're no company at all."

She watched the goldfish swimming back and forth. "If you had any ambition, you'd get a job and make something of yourself."

The smile faded from her lips as she retrieved her coffee cup and sat on the sofa facing the fire. Was that what life was all about? Making something of yourself? Or was her mother closer to the truth? Accept and be happy. But what did it take to be happy?

Reaching deep within her memories, Sam forced herself to examine uncomfortable areas she'd previously shied from. How did she truly feel about being Frank Adams' successor at Adams Air? She turned the question over in her mind, discovering with mild surprise that she really had never wanted anything else. Despite the pressures and disappointments, she was doing what she loved to do. The rewards far outweighed any small dissatisfactions.

Although she tried, Sam couldn't think of anything else she would enjoy as much. Adams Air had problems, certainly, but what business didn't? And she was holding her own. Better than that, she was making progress. For every account she'd lost, she was adding two. And that felt good.

But was Adams Air enough? Could she be happy devoting the rest of her life to freight sheets and ledger pages? Alone?

No.

Biting her lip, Sam concentrated on the problem that immediately surfaced in her mind. The more successful she became, the less likely she was to trust any man who displayed an interest in her. She would view his attentions as an attempt to control her business. This was the core of her uncertainty with Luke; it could only grow worse as Adams Air expanded.

There didn't seem to be a comfortable solution. If she wanted a relationship, then at some point she would have to trust her man's intentions.

The thought led her uneasily toward the question she had resolutely refused to examine.

Had she accused Luke unjustly?

Why wouldn't he be interested in and excited about Adams Air? Flying was his primary interest— air freight was his future, with or without Sam Adams. Wasn't it possible that he was interested in Sam *and* her company? Wasn't it possible that Adams Air was no more to him than a delightful bonus?

Yes. Sam rubbed her temples. The bottom line was that she knew he wasn't the type of man to use a woman for his own gain.

Once she admitted this, she also had to admit she had always known it. She had been running away, afraid to trust Luke's love, afraid to trust her own heart. Whenever she had felt love's vulnerability, she had thrown up a shield of suspicion and made herself believe it.

Dear God, was it that simple? And that complicated?

Sam's wide eyes swung toward the telephone and she willed it to ring. When it remained silent, she dropped her head to the back of the sofa and closed her damp eyes. Luke wouldn't call. His pride and his anger stood in the way. And she didn't blame him; she had said unforgivable things.

She had destroyed the love she wanted with all her heart. And now she had to live with what she'd done.

*   *   *

"Well, tonight's the night. Are you going to wish me luck?" Sam glanced into the mirror on the back of her office door and retied the soft silk bow at her throat. The rose-colored silk softened the severity of her gray wool suit. Careful makeup concealed the shadows beneath her eyes; she wore her hair twisted up into a businesslike knot.

"Consolidated Bakeries?" Marva asked, lighting a cigarette.

"Hmmm. If we get that account, I'll never again worry about the end of the month."

"That big, huh?"

"That big." Sam stepped back from the mirror and frowned, wishing she hadn't spent half of the previous night sitting before the fire avoiding her lonely bed. "How do I look?"

"You look gorgeous. As usual." Marva tilted her head and considered. "Maybe a little tired."

"What would you say if I told you I've decided to take a vacation next month?"

"I'd say I was witnessing a miracle. I don't think you've taken a day off since I've known you." Marva straightened in her chair and smiled. "Are you sure this place can get along without you?"

Sam laughed. "You'll probably get along better."

"I doubt that. But we'll manage. What brought this on?"

Sam reached for a gray coat that matched her suit. "There's more to life than work."

Marva stared. "Would you mind saying that again? I thought I heard you say there was more to life than work."

Grimacing, Sam tried for a smile. "Have I been that rigid and compulsive?"

"Worse."

"I think it's time I aimed toward a better balance in my life."

"Agreed." Marva's gaze traveled to Sam's hand. "Would this balance include a certain man who bears a startling resemblance to a gentleman who has been appearing frequently on late-night TV?"

"I don't think so, Marva." She'd seen the TV movies too, watching them with an aching mixture of pain and longing. "Things were said that can't be unsaid. I—I'm afraid that bridge is burned."

"I'm sorry, Sam."

"So am I." Turning aside so Marva couldn't see the torture in her eyes, she made an effort to keep her voice light. After patting Marva's ample shoulder, Sam almost ran to her car, welcoming the cold, wintry air on her hot cheeks. Whenever she thought about Luke, about stupidly losing him, the tears were only a heartbeat away. Resolutely, she focused her mind on the upcoming appointment.

The restaurant where she was to meet the president of Consolidated Bakeries for drinks was new and difficult to find. When Sam finally spotted the restaurant's small sign, she released a quick sound of irritation. She was late. She didn't like after-hours appointments to begin with: the time usually coincided with rush-hour traffic and practically guaranteed that she'd be late or have to wait. She hoped Mr. March hadn't been waiting long.

Inside, she glanced about the restaurant, noting a decor that affected a self-conscious charm, then she hurried toward the bar, feeling rushed and slightly off balance. At the entrance to a large, dim room comfortably furnished with deep easy chairs grouped around intimate tables, Sam paused and drew a long breath. It wouldn't do to appear rattled and flustered. Not after she had practiced her presentation until it was letter-perfect and smoothly professional. Consolidated Bakeries was a vital opportunity, and she had to empty her thoughts of anything but business.

After touching her hair and straightening the silk bow at her throat, Sam lifted her chin and strode into the room, confident that Adams Air and Samantha Adams were exactly what Consolidated Bakeries needed.

The first person she saw was Luke Bannister.

Chapter Fifteen

Sam couldn't think; she couldn't breathe. Somehow she stumbled through the introductions, meeting Ed March and his assistant. She even managed to order a drink. But all she could think of were the vivid blue eyes that swept her face with a hungry eagerness, then turned coolly distant. The world seemed to drop away, leaving only an acute awareness of the man in the chair next to her—nothing else existed or mattered. Her stomach tightened painfully and her nerves leaped to the surface of her skin.

". . . an apology to you both."

Sam blinked and tried desperately to focus on what Ed March was saying. This was the dream account; the account of a lifetime. But no matter how desperately she tried to follow Ed March's words, her mind centered on Luke's politely casual greeting, his cool gaze. Her senses reeled with the scent of his spiced after-shave; she stared helplessly at his strong bronzed hand gripping his drink.

"Mr. Ryan is new to our company and he should have checked immediately to ascertain whether either of your companies had the capacity to handle our plans for expansion."

Sam closed her eyes. She had to pay attention. Lifting her drink in trembling fingers, she swallowed deeply, hoping the sharp bite of icy liquid would clear her thoughts. Oh Luke, Luke. Look at me, she pleaded silently. Look at me as you did before.

She darted a glance toward him, and found him absorbed in what March was saying. Her gaze lingered lovingly on his strong profile, drinking in the silver streak at his temple, the clean powerful line of his jaw. Oh God, what had she done?

No business was more essential than loving and being loved. How could she ever have been such a fool as to think so? When she looked at him, all the obstacles she'd invented seemed so foolishly small and unimportant. She could no longer recall what items she had found more compelling than Luke's arms, than his wide, warm mouth.

". . . so, I'm afraid we've wasted your time. What we're looking for is a company about the size of Bannister and Adams Air combined. I'm terribly sorry if we inconvenienced either of you."

The account was lost and Sam was too numb to care. She heard herself murmuring something incomprehensible. Ed March leaned to shake her hand and she smiled woodenly and nodded and murmured polite responses. "It's quite all right, I understand perfectly." And, "It was no trouble at all. These things happen." And finally, "It was a pleasure to meet you too."

March and his assistant moved toward the exit, leaving Sam and Luke standing beside their table. Sam's breath emerged with difficulty, she felt her heart accelerate painfully. Slowly she turned to face him, yearning toward lips she remembered so well, toward arms that had sheltered her from the cold. They stood a scant foot apart and only the studied distance in his eyes prevented her from collapsing into his arms.

"How are you, Sam?"

His deep voice raced through her body like a physical touch. Sam moistened her lips. "Fine," she whispered.

"A tough one to lose."

"Yes."

His hand lifted at his side, then dropped. "Well, I don't want to keep you . . ." Bending, he lifted his topcoat and folded it over his arm.

He was treating her like a casual business acquaintance. Sam couldn't bear it. "Luke . . ." He couldn't just walk away, she couldn't allow it. Maybe if she explained, maybe if they talked . . . Her hand jumped to the sleeve of his blue suit and she gazed up at him, her heart in her eyes. "I'm in no hurry. Would you like another drink?"

For a moment she thought he would accept, she thought it would be all right. Then something like pain flashed across his gaze and his mouth tightened. "I have a lot of work to do tonight."

He was going to leave! Sam swallowed hard. "Can I give you a lift to the airport?" Please God, let him say yes.

"Thanks, but I'm staying at the Ramada across the street." His wide mouth curved in a sudden grin. "You don't happen to have an appointment with Zimmerman Sugar tomorrow morning, do you?"

"No. I've never heard of Zimmerman Sugar." Her voice was dulled by disappointment and by the pain of knowing he didn't want her.

"Good. After the beating we took tonight, I don't think I'd be eager to go up against you tomorrow. Especially not since I told you how to beat me."

She sensed he was trying to keep their conversation light and impersonal. The knowledge tore at her heart. "Luke, please." Pride came tumbling down. "Can we talk?"

"I think we've said it all, haven't we, Sam? You were right and I was wrong. It wouldn't work."

He gazed down at her and she felt like crying out at the terrible finality she saw in his eyes and heard in his deep voice. His hand rose and for a breathless instant, Sam thought he would stroke her cheek. But he touched his tie instead. He stared at her and opened his lips to speak, then apparently thought better of it and closed his mouth in a smile that didn't quite reach his eyes.

"Goodnight, Sam."

Her knees buckled and she sat abruptly, watching him walk out of the door and out of her life.

The waitress winked at her. "Wow. What a hunk, huh? I wonder what lucky girl he's going home to." The waitress removed the men's glasses. "Want another drink, honey? You look like you could use one."

Numb, Sam nodded.

People entered the bar and departed in a blur. Sam sat before her untouched drink and stared at nothing and tried to think past the ache throbbing in her heart. It was over. It was really over.

Her gaze swept the noisy bar and gradually focused on the smiling couples swinging through the door arm in arm. It was a couples world, a world of pairs. Sam had never felt as lonely in her life.

It seemed that everyone else had what she had thrown away. She had stupidly rejected the one man who made her feel warm inside and cherished. A man who loosened the knots of her rigidity and had released an exhilarating spontaneity that she hadn't experienced before or since. A man whose strengths and weaknesses meshed with hers to form a strong unit. A man who had loved her from the first moment.

A man who was just across the street.

Sam's eyes darkened and her spine straightened. Was she going to let him walk out of her life? Was she that weak? Luke Bannister loved her and she loved him. And dammit, she was not going to allow her stupidity to wreck their future.

She was going to talk to him and he was going to listen, that's all there was to it. And she wouldn't quit until he forgave her. If it took the rest of her life, she'd find a way to have the one thing she wanted most.

Standing, Sam slipped into her coat and her jaw firmed stubbornly. If Bannister refused to see her—and she wouldn't blame him if he did—then she would phone him. And then she'd write him. She'd wear him down. She would show Luke Bannister the meaning of persistence.

A determined smile illuminated her face. She loved him. And Samantha Adams never gave up when she wanted something.

Ducking her head against the cold night wind, she ran across the street and asked the Ramada desk clerk the number of Bannister's room. Then she stepped into the elevator and swallowed hard.

What if he closed the door in her face? What if he wouldn't talk to her? Panic raced along her nerves and she quelled it with effort. Luke loved her; she had to trust in that. He had loved her from the first.

Love didn't vanish overnight; it wasn't something one turned on and off like a water tap. She reminded herself of this as she stood before his door and drew a deep breath for courage. He still loved her; he just had to. She lifted a shaking hand and knocked.

It seemed to take forever before the door opened and Luke Bannister filled the frame. He still wore his tie but his shirt sleeves were rolled to the elbow and his black hair fell across his forehead as if he'd just run his fingers through it. His dark eyebrow lifted and he stared down at her with surprise.

"Sam? Is something wrong?"

Sam drew a breath. "Bannister, I sure hope you

like the looks of me, because I'm going to marry you." She smiled up at him, her eyes steady and sure.

Wearily, he passed a hand over his face. "Don't do this, Sam. I'm in no mood for jokes."

"This is no joke and it's not a phony line. I intend to marry you." She pushed past him and strode into his room, hoping she appeared more confident than she felt. She paused beside the papers strewn across a small table, then turned to face him.

"Sam, as you pointed out, we have a lot of problems . . ."

"We'll work them out. I love you, Bannister. And you love me. That's all that matters."

"This isn't what you thought a few weeks ago."

"I was a fool." She pulled off her coat and deliberately dropped it on the floor, resisting the urge to hang it neatly over a chair back. "And I apologize."

Luke stared at the gray heap on the carpet. He closed the door and stepped farther into the room. "I love to fly and you hate it."

"So you fly and I'll stay home."

"What about me stealing your business?"

"You don't have to steal it, Bannister. I'm giving it to you." She pulled the pins from her hair and shook a cloud of dark waves down around her shoulders. "On the condition that I handle all the paperwork. And I'm going to drive you mad by insisting on flight plans and insurance. You supervise the pilots and fly old *Louise* or *Harriet* or whoever."

Something moved deep in his eyes and the ghost of a smile touched the corners of his lips as he watched her hair tumble toward the slope of her breast. "What are you doing, Sam?"

Her heart soared. Suddenly, she knew it was going to be all right. "I'm seducing you."

"It's working." Slowly, he loosened his tie, then laid it on the bureau top. Neatly. His fingers paused at his shirt buttons. "Are you going to expect me to take orders from you?"

Sam tugged the silk bow at her throat, her eyes on the patch of dark hair emerging from his shirt. "Absolutely. And I'll take orders from you when it concerns the pilots or the planes."

"Agreed." He pulled his shirt from his pants, his eyes sweeping to the creamy swell above her lacy bra as Sam opened her blouse then carelessly dropped it near her coat. His voice roughened. "Darlin', this is and always will be love at first sight. And you don't believe in love at first sight."

She saw the desire darkening his wonderful eyes, saw his need for her rising strong and hard. "I do now." Her fingers fumbled at the zipper to her skirt.

He slid his belt out of the loops and coiled it over his hand then laid it neatly beside his tie. "I'll drive you up a wall by forgetting things. I couldn't tell you right this minute where my spare socks are."

"We'll compromise. You'll be neater and I'll be less rigid." Sam wiggled sensuously out of her skirt and kicked it aside, her heart leaping at his quick intake of breath.

"We'll drive each other crazy, darlin', you know that." His shoes and socks followed his slacks. Stark naked, he folded his pants over a hanger.

Sam slid out of her nylons, tossing them toward a chair, and faced him, loving the sight of his strong, muscled body. "I don't care. I don't care if you've lost your socks or if you want to spend every weekend flying. I only care that you love me. I want to spend the rest of my life nagging you about details."

"You are the most beautiful woman I've ever seen," he said hoarsely, his eyes traveling over her breasts and hips.

Sam laughed softly, her eyes shining. "You keep telling me and maybe someday I'll believe it."

He stepped forward and crushed her into his arms, buring his face in her hair. "I'm going to tell you every day for the rest of your life. God, Sam, I've missed you every hour of every day!"

"I never believed I could hurt so much. Oh Luke, I was so foolish!"

"Don't you know there aren't any problems that you and I together can't solve?"

She leaned back in his arms and looked up at him. "We'll take them one at a time and find solutions we can both live with." Kisses teased over her temples, her eyelids, her throat. "I'll pay the bills and keep the books. You manage scheduling."

"I'll cook the steaks. You cook those casserole things."

His hands slid over her breasts and Sam moaned softly, her skin on fire. "I'll throw newspapers on the floor if you'll put the cap on the toothpaste."

"I'll fly the planes and you keep them filled." He raised his mouth from her lips and smiled down at her. "I'll make the kids and you keep track of them."

She ran her trembling hands over his chest and laughed softly, then looked into his smoldering eyes and felt weak with joy. "I love you, Luke Bannister. With all my heart, I love you."

Luke swept her into his arms and carried her to the bed. Then his wide, strong hands framed her face and he looked down into her eyes. "Keep loving me, Sam. I need you so much."

Sam circled his neck with her arms and pulled him close, close enough to feel their hearts beating as one. She kissed his chin and smiled. "What do you think of the name, Ad-Ban Freight Company?"

He grinned down at her. "How about Ban-Ad?"

She laughed softly, her dark eyes radiant with

happiness. "On second thought, maybe something like Consolidated Air would be better."

"See how easy it is?"

Then his lips covered hers and the wonder of loving him swept away all the unimportant thoughts.

RAPTURE ROMANCE
BOOK CLUB
❧

*Bringing You The World of
Love and Romance With
Three Exclusive Book Lines*

RAPTURE ROMANCE · SIGNET REGENCY
ROMANCE · SCARLET RIBBONS

**Subscribe to Rapture Romance
and have your choice of two
Rapture Romance Book Club Packages.**

- **PLAN A:** Four Rapture Romances plus two Signet Regency Romances for just $9.75!

- **PLAN B:** Four Rapture Romances, one Signet Regency Romance and one Scarlet Ribbons Romance for just $10.45!

Whichever package you choose, you save 60 cents off the combined cover prices plus you get a FREE Rapture Romance.

"THAT'S A SAVINGS OF $2.55
OFF THE COMBINED
COVER PRICES"

We're so sure you'll love them, we'll give you 10 days to look over the set you choose at home. Then you can keep the set or return the books and owe nothing.

To start you off, we'll send you four books absolutely **FREE**. Our two latest Rapture Romances plus our latest Signet Regency and our latest Scarlet Ribbons. The total value of all four books is $9.10, but they're yours **FREE** even if you never buy another book.

To get your books, use the convenient coupon on the following page.

YOUR FIRST FOUR BOOKS
ARE FREE

Mail the Coupon below

Please send me the Four Books described **FREE** and without obligation. Unless you hear from me after I receive them, please send me 6 New Books to review each month. I have indicated below which plan I would like to be sent. I understand that you will bill me for only 5 books as I always get a Rapture Romance Novel **FREE** plus an additional 60¢ off, making a total savings of $2.55 each month. I will be billed no shipping, handling or other charges. There is no minimum number of books I must buy, and I can cancel at any time. The first 4 FREE books are mine to keep even if I never buy another book.

   Check the Plan you would like.

   ☐ **PLAN A:** Four Rapture Romances plus two Signet Regency Romances for just $9.75 each month.

   ☐ **PLAN B:** Four Rapture Romances plus one Signet Regency Romance and one Scarlet Ribbons for just $10.45 each month.

NAME _____
                              (please print)

ADDRESS _____ CITY _____

STATE _____ ZIP _____ SIGNATURE _____
                                          (if under 18, parent or guardian must sign)

Rapture Romance

This offer, limited to one per household and not valid to present subscribers, expires June 30, 1984. Prices subject to change. Specific titles subject to availability. Allow a minimum of 4 weeks for delivery.

RAPTURE ROMANCE

Provocative and sensual, passionate and tender— the magic and mystery of love in all its many guises

Coming next month

DELINQUENT DESIRE by Carla Neggers. Meeting at a summer camp for delinquent girls, it was unlikely that cool executive Casey Gray and Hollywood agent Jeff Coldwell would give themselves to each other so freely, so passionately. Both shared an unusual secret in their pasts, but by the time the secrets were revealed, it was too late—Casey had lost her cool . . . and her heart. . . .

A SECURE ARRANGEMENT by JoAnn Robb. Jillian Tara Kennedy wasn't prepared for aggressive, seductive Travis Tyrell, who awakened a passion within her she couldn't deny. And even though she'd sworn never to be dependent on any man, Travis' silky caresses broke down her resistance, until she was fighting not his desire, but her own. . . .

ON WINGS OF DESIRE by Jillian Roth. Alaskan bush pilot Erinne Parker was intrigued by mysterious biologist Jansen Lancaster. But being swept into a blazing affair with him only confused her more, and made her wonder if she was learning to love him . . . only to have him leave her. . . .

LADY IN FLIGHT by Diana Morgan. At his first touch, sculptor Sabrina Melendey knew her heart belonged totally to scientist Colin Forrester. But they were as far apart as art and science, and Sabrina didn't believe that love could conquer all. . . .

RAPTURE ROMANCE

Provocative and sensual, passionate and tender— the magic and mystery of love in all its many guises

New Titles Available Now

(0451)

#65 ☐ **WISH ON A STAR by Katherine Ransom.** Fighting for independence from her rich, domineering father, Vanessa Hamilton fled to Maine—and into the arms of Rory McGee. Drawn to his strong masculinity, his sensuous kisses ignited her soul. But she had only just tasted her new-found freedom—was she willing to give herself to another forceful man?
(129083—$1.95)*

#66 ☐ **FLIGHT OF FANCY by Maggie Osborne.** A plane crash brought Samantha Adams and Luke Bannister together for a short, passionate time. But they were rivals in the air freight business, and even though Luke said he loved her and wanted to marry her, Samantha was unsure. Did Luke really want her— or was he only after Adams Air Freight? (128702—$1.95)*

#67 ☐ **ENCHANTED ENCORE by Rosalynn Carroll.** Vicki Owens couldn't resist Patrick Wallingford's fiery embrace years ago, and now he was back reawakening a tantalizing ecstasy. Could she believe love was forever the second time around, or was he only using her to make another woman jealous?
(128710—$1.95)*

#68 ☐ **A PUBLIC AFFAIR by Eleanor Frost.** Barbara Danbury told herself not to trust rising political star Morgan Newman. But she was lost when he pledged his love to her in a night of passion. Then scandal shattered Morgan's ideal image and suddenly Barbara doubted everything—except her burning hunger for him. . . . (128729—$1.95)*

*Price is $2.25 in Canada
To order, use the convenient coupon on the last page.

RAPTURE ROMANCE

*Provocative and sensual,
passionate and tender—
the magic and mystery of love
in all its many guises*

**Buy them at your local

bookstore or use coupon

on next page for ordering.**

RAPTURE ROMANCE

Provocative and sensual, passionate and tender— the magic and mystery of love in all its many guises

(0451)

#45	☐	SEPTEMBER SONG by Lisa Moore.	(126301—$1.95)*
#46	☐	A MOUNTAIN MAN by Megan Ashe.	(126319—$1.95)*
#47	☐	THE KNAVE OF HEARTS by Estelle Edwards.	(126327—$1.95)*
#48	☐	BEYOND ALL STARS by Linda McKenzie.	(126335—$1.95)*
#49	☐	DREAMLOVER by JoAnn Robb.	(126343—$1.95)*
#50	☐	A LOVE SO FRESH by Marilyn Davids.	(126351—$1.95)*
#51	☐	LOVER IN THE WINGS by Francine Shore.	(127617—$1.95)*
#52	☐	SILK AND STEEL by Kathryn Kent.	(127625—$1.95)*
#53	☐	ELUSIVE PARADISE by Eleanor Frost.	(127633—$1.95)*
#54	☐	RED SKY AT NIGHT by Ellie Winslow.	(127641—$1.95)*
#55	☐	BITTERSWEET TEMPTATION by Jillian Roth.	(127668—$1.95)*
#56	☐	SUN SPARK by Nina Coombs.	(127676—$1.95)*

*Price is $2.25 in Canada.

Buy them at your local bookstore or use this convenient coupon for ordering.

NEW AMERICAN LIBRARY
P.O. Box 999, Bergenfield, New Jersey 07621

Please send me the books I have checked above. I am enclosing $_____ (please add $1.00 to this order to cover postage and handling). Send check or money order—no cash or C.O.D.'s. Prices and numbers are subject to change without notice.

Name_____

Address_____

City _____ State _____ Zip Code _____

Allow 4-6 weeks for delivery.
This offer is subject to withdrawal without notice.

RAPTURE ROMANCE

Provocative and sensual, passionate and tender— the magic and mystery of love in all its many guises

Buy them at your local
bookstore or use coupon
on next page for ordering.